Time Travelers, Ghosts, and Other Visitors

Time Travelers, Ghosts, and Other Visitors

Nina Kiriki Hoffman

Five Star • Waterville, Maine

First Edition, Second Printing.

Published in 2003 in conjunction with
Tekno Books and Ed Gorman.

Set in 11 pt. Plantin.

Printed in the United States on permanent paper.

Library of Congress Cataloging-in-Publication Data

Hoffman, Nina Kiriki.
    Time travelers, ghosts, and other visitors : fiction / by
Nina Kiriki Hoffman.—1st ed.
        p. cm.
    The skeleton key—Objects of desire—Unleashed—Mint
condition—Night life—Entertaining possibilities—
Toobychubbies—Haunted humans—Egg shells.
    ISBN 0-7862-5338-X (hc : alk. paper)
    1. Fantasy fiction, American. I. Title.
PS3558.O34624T56 2003
813'.54—dc21   2003040865

Dedication

To all my editors. Thanks.

Table of Contents

Introduction

Nina Kiriki Hoffman's stories seldom follow the regulation literary standards and practices of taking an ordinary character, throwing him or her into extraordinary life-altering circumstances, and then watching as that character sorts things out. The people in Nina's stories are seldom ordinary. More often than not, they are utterly charming but downright weird folks who are forced to confront odd and unexpected problems that result in innovative and frequently poignant solutions. Each tale is startling in its originality; in a NKH story, you're likely to lose the bet if you try to predict what might happen next. Her work is unique in its quirk, compassion, and wit.

Nina's stories take traditional literary tropes and turn them on their hair-tufted, pointy, fairytale ears. We've all read stories in which a woman is forced to confront her painful past, but nothing quite like the story of Tess in "The Skeleton Key," a story that explores the confrontation between good and evil and gives Hermes the airtime he so richly deserves. The story (a Nebula nominee) examines faith, betrayal, sacrifice, and leads to the discovery that resolution is possible once we unlock those things that keep us trapped in hurt and pain.

The new mother in "Unleashed" who hates and fears what she has become because being "Unleashed" gives her access to a forbidden and uncontrolled world. The narrator of "Entertaining Possibilities" is something of a magical actuary, who faces a situation familiar to many of us: the in-laws who don't believe we're a good enough mate for their little darling. The twist in this story is that the in-laws wield powers that leave the narrator scratching his head to ask what would Darrin Stevens do (WWDSD)?

"Toobychubbies" is a satire about the dangers of allowing television to be a substitute for good parenting. In Nina's fertile imagination, the boob tube becomes an instrument of doom in the hands of enemy invaders. It's a modern day horror story that doesn't shy away from addressing hard issues, like the willing complicity in evil undertakings, as the story asks just how much would a harried mother give for an extra hour of sleep?

The ghosts in "Haunted Humans" (another Nebula nominee) serve as both literal and symbolic beings, rooted in the past, but with a powerful hold on the present. The story is part mystery, part self-help manual, part ghost story, part something that has no name, and my favorite in the collection.

Nina's stories reveal lush settings, lovingly decorated by one of the field's most innovative literary interior designers and landscape architects. Her work is touching, funny, compelling, and original. How lucky you are to be holding her newest collection of short fiction in your hands. I invite you to turn the page and read on.

Leslie What
Summer 2003

The Skeleton Key

Blood is the ink in which we write the meaning of our lives.

I didn't discover this until after I died. That was when the scribbles I had made with my blood while living became legible, and I had reason to thank the god I had consecrated myself to.

By the time I was thirteen I knew Hermes was my favorite god. My mom had read me the D'Aulaires book of Greek myths when I was eight, and I had memorized all the pictures and most of the myths pretty soon after that. At ten I got my new best friend Sasha to read the book, and though we were attracted to Artemis and Athena, we loved Hermes best. We were obsessed with things Greek after that. Our thirteenth Halloween, instead of trick-or-treating, Sasha and I snuck off to the hill back of Lindley Farm.

The air was full of frost and wood smoke and mischief. We wore our winter coats, hats, gloves and scarves. Sasha carried a canteen half-full of red wine she had stolen from her parents' liquor cabinet. I had a saucepan, some charcoal briquettes, and a little piece of raw flank steak. We had thought about using candles to light our way, but it was too windy and somebody might see us, so we each had a flashlight.

Near the top of the hill, not far off the hiking trail, lurked a clearing. We pushed our way through bushes to get there. Between sentinel trees with bare branches, we scuffed new-fallen leaves aside with our boots to bare the earth to the constellations, and sat on the damp ground. I set the charcoal on a flat rock and managed to light it without extra lighter fluid (I'd dosed it before I left the house).

Sasha and I did our Greek things: she poured a libation of wine on the earth, dedicating it to all the Olympians, after which we took a comradely sip and winced at the tongue-drying alcoholic taste. I scorched the steak over the coals, saying I hoped the fragrance of the smoke would nourish the gods. We chanted a chant we had devised with many erasings and lots of note-passing in history class, which was the most boring class we had, with the least attentive teacher. Our chant was full of careful phrases about how all the gods were great and yet we wanted one of them in particular to watch over us, if that wouldn't offend the rest of them too much (in Greek myths many people appeared to have patron gods, so it didn't seem out of line to ask for it).

We slashed our thumbs with a razor blade I had taken from my dad's medicine cabinet, squeezed out a drop of blood each on the ground (thanking Gaea), pressed our wounds together, and declared that we belonged to the Sisterhood of Hermes.

Sasha's blood was cold and so was mine, but with our fingers pressed together I felt warmth, even though the rest of my hand was freezing. I saw a falling star above me and suddenly my arms prickled, with hair standing on end. I glanced at Sasha. It was too dark for me to see what she was thinking behind her face. Neither of us breathed for a moment. A flower of warmth blossomed in my chest.

"Tess?" Sasha murmured.

"Yes," I whispered, but that was all we said.

At last we separated our hands. I started breathing again, and my sense of the mystery in everything went away, but I remembered how it had felt.

Coming down the hill, Sasha and I were silent. We never did talk about it directly, but we continued to act as if the Sisterhood were real.

We taught ourselves the Greek alphabet to the extent of using it as a replacement code for regular letters, and we wrote notes to each other we had trouble decoding. We met once a month and snuck off to our hill, no matter what the weather, and performed rituals we made up, sometimes stealing bits from things we found in the encyclopedia or myth books. It was the best secret we had ever had. Often I felt the silence come over me, the sense that something was listening to us and responding. Sometimes we received signs that our prayers were answered: Sasha got an A on a test she barely studied for; I got the bike I wanted for my fourteenth birthday; we both got dates for school dances; and Sasha found a five-dollar bill on the sidewalk.

It was as close as I got to religion.

By the time I was sixteen, the words "Hermes help me" came out of my mouth instead of cuss words whenever the situation warranted an exclamation, and I didn't even notice. Mom stopped commenting on it after the novelty wore off; Dad had never even noticed.

When we were seventeen, Sasha, who had skipped a grade in junior high, left for college. In our letters we never talked about the Sisterhood; she was never home at the right time of month for ritual, and I didn't know if she did something about it where she was. I continued to go to the hilltop to offer fire, wine, words, and the incense of burning meat to the open sky, but I felt lonely without Sasha. The mystery seemed more distant.

Sasha had gone on to the University, but my grade point average and my ambitions weren't as high as hers. She planned to be a psychologist. I didn't know what I wanted, so when I got out of high school, I decided to settle for General Studies at State, and see if anything excited me. Sasha's letters got shorter and shorter and mostly talked about the fact that she had to study a lot now so she didn't have time to write. I talked about my excitement when I moved into my own studio apartment and how weird it was when Mom and Dad were right across town.

Then I met Steve.

If I had seen highlights of my first college semester in a horror movie, I would have been yelling at the girl on screen not to be such an idiot. I mean, it's like when people split up to search the scary house with all the lights off—you know: stupid.

But I was just me, and Steve was just a great-looking curly-haired guy from the coffee shop who invited me to his apartment a couple of times. We had a great time at his place. We rented horror movies and ordered out for pizza and played Monster in the Closet after we turned off the TV.

So when he invited me to a Halloween party where there would be a lot of other people like him, I thought it was a terrific idea. Of the four guys I had dated so far in college, Steve was the most fun. If there were more people like him, I was ready to meet them. As long as I got home before midnight, so I could celebrate my fifth anniversary of the Sisterhood up on Lindley Hill. I put a twenty in my pocket for cab fare in case Steve didn't want to leave when I did.

Only he didn't take me to somebody's house; he took me to an abandoned church.

"It's awfully dark," I said when we drove up to the building, which was on the outskirts of town without even a streetlight near it. The only light came from the building itself, a flickering behind broken stained glass windows.

"It's that kind of party, Tess," Steve said, ushering me in

14

through big wooden double doors and barring them behind us.

I began to feel suspicious and just a little sick around then, because beyond the entry hall, in the church's chapel, stood a circle of fat lighted black candles on the flagstone floor, and around the circle of light stood a circle of people in dark hooded robes, and on the far wall hung a big black cross, upside down.

The air smelled of *patchouli* and singed hair.

In the center of the circles of light and people, there was a black slab about six feet long and three feet wide, with shackles attached. It was crusted with something dark and flaky.

I glanced up at the windows. The faces had been broken out of all the saints.

"Hermes help me," I muttered.

They dressed me in a white gown. A young woman with green eyes combed out my hair before they shackled me to the stained stone.

They told me no one would hear me scream, and I tested it and discovered they were right.

They told me Satan would be pleased with me, that each act of humiliation, degradation, and cruelty they practiced on me would bring them power; and that my ultimate sacrifice of blood and life would bring them extreme power. And in the end, they were wrong.

When at last I wept, voiceless, an aching in some parts of me, sharp shocks in others, burning and throbbing elsewhere, when at last Steve drew a knife and spilled my heart's blood, the god came to us in the guise of a dark-haired boy, his *chlamys* draped carelessly over one shoulder and fastened at the other. In his hand he held the *caduceus*, his wand of sleep and balm of healing, with serpents twined about it.

"I'm sorry I'm late," he said.

Steve had given me a slow but fatal wound. It was a relief, actually, because they stopped torturing me and just waited for me to die. I was still aware enough to see that all the black-robed people fell to the ground. One started a chant, "Bless us, Lord Satan," and all the others joined in.

He glanced at them, but walked through their circle and came to kneel on the slab beside me. "I'm sorry," he said again. Pearly light haloed him. I couldn't figure out if it was my sight going or something that was actually happening. "I'm sorry," he said, touching the smaller wounds. As he touched them, the pain faded from them. "There was so little energy for me in this era that it took your great sacrifice for me to manifest. I would not have had you die for me."

My eyelids were getting heavier, and pain no longer pinned me in place.

"Not against your will," he murmured, putting his hands in the blood on my chest.

I shaped my mouth around the breath coming out of me. "Much rather you than any other," I whispered. Wonder battled the lassitude seeping into me.

"Bless us, Lord Satan. Bless us, Lord Satan," they cried all around us.

He leaned over and pressed his lips to mine, and in that moment, all pain faded and I came free of my body, which stopped breathing. He rose and held out his hand, which glowed with my blood as if it were rosy liquid light. Confused, I reached toward him—how could I do that without a body?—and saw my own arm, a phantom but there, as I held it out.

"Come," he said, taking my hand. I felt a tingling warmth in my palm and fingers where his hand touched mine. The pearly haze wrapped around him was very strong now. We walked out past all the kneeling dark figures. I glanced back once. My body, violated, burned, stabbed, its face twisted with pain, lay in its own blood and fluids. I shuddered and walked through the wall hand in hand with my god.

We traveled to a place removed from the earth I had spent my life on, yet just around the corner. We sat in a midnight meadow where all the grasses glowed with green pinpoints of light, and night-blooming flowers offered cores of yellow radiance and golden scent to the stars. From somewhere not too far away, a stream whispered and murmured.

"I am the god of travelers," he said, "I am the conductor of souls; I can take you to the next world."

"But I—" I began, then stopped, my fingers touching my throat, surprised at having a voice again. They had gripped my tongue in red-hot pinchers, and my screams had left my throat torn and raw; but that pain was gone now.

He waited, smiling at me, so beautiful I wanted to hug him, the image of my dreams and wishes.

"I don't feel ready," I said. Though I didn't know what I meant.

"You can stay for a while," he murmured. "It won't be the same."

After a silence, I touched his knee.

He put his hand on mine, closed his fingers around my hand. "Do you wish to go back into your dirt? I have done such a thing before."

"My body, you mean?" I asked. I thought of my last sight of my body: hurt, mangled, wretched. "No!" Heat flowed through me as I remembered candlelit faces framed in black hoods. A smile from a brown-eyed woman as she leaned down to flay some skin off my arm. The frowning concentration of a man with deep crows'-feet at the outer edges of his eyes as he sketched a design on my stomach with many prickings of a hot needle. "No," I said, "but I don't want to leave Earth. And I—Lord, those people tortured me . . ." I stared at my free hand. Each bone in each finger had been broken, yet now my hand looked whole.

"Yes," he said.

"And, Lord, I want to hurt them."

"It will pass," he said after a little while, gripping my hand gently.

"Is it wrong for me to want that?"

"You must want what you want," he said. "I can help you with some things. Vengeance is not one of my attributes. If it is in your heart to search out and punish all who have harmed you . . ." He looked away. "I can grant you certain powers. Then you will have to use them as you deem best."

We stood in front of my parents' house. Something in me had called me Home, here, not to my apartment, where I had only lived six months. His hands lay on my shoulders, warm, comforting. I could feel strength flowing from them. "Tess," he murmured. "You need never be alone now. When you are ready to travel, call me and I'll come for you."

"What if I'm not ready but I just . . . need you?"

"Call." He turned me. He embraced me. He faded away.

I clutched the key he had given me. I wanted to be three places at once:

I wanted to be alive and walking up the path to my parents' house, so I could knock on the door and Mom would answer and I could fall into her arms.

I wanted to be with Sasha, telling her that we had been right all along, that there really was a force, that it heard us when we spoke to it.

I wanted to be in the abandoned church.

I wanted to be alive and terrible in the church, slicing all those people open, shedding their blood in the name of my Lord, making him stronger at their expense.

Though when I really thought about it, I knew that wouldn't work, any more than their sacrifice of me had worked; I was already promised to Another. They, too, had made their choice.

The wind rose, carrying papers down the street. I felt it against my hair, the faintest tickle of breath.

I walked up the path to my parents' sleeping house.

The curtains to most of the rooms were closed, but through a gap in the living room curtains I saw Dad's recliner with sections of newspaper scattered near it, left the way he had dropped them earlier as he searched out Mom's byline, and Mom's recliner with a stack of blue books on the table next to it, one opened: she had been reading the work of Dad's high school students. They spent their evenings talking about work. I had heard it all my life, the excitement Dad felt finding a story in the paper Mom hadn't told him she was working on, his patient suspense as she searched through a stack of exercise papers for the one he thought was a gem. Often she saw things in his students' work that didn't impress him until she pointed them out to him. Sometimes he mentioned an angle she hadn't thought of in her search for story, and she would address it in the follow-up story. They both valued the fresh eyes of each other.

I wondered how they would see me.

I stood on the porch, thinking about walking through walls the way I had seen ghosts in movies do, wondering. I put my hand on the door and pushed. There was initial resistance. I pushed harder, felt the door against my palm: not solid, really; like water on the verge of freezing, without the cold. I leaned against the door and gradually it parted somehow, its

19

matter moved to either side, and I was in the front hall.

"That takes too long," I muttered. I turned back and jumped at the door. I bumped my chin and scuffed my palms and bounced back into the front hall. "Ouch! Hermes help me!"

"What is it?" he asked, standing beside me.

"Oh. Excuse me. Why is it so hard to walk through things?"

"Did you ask first?"

"What?"

"Everything has its own spirit, Tess. Homes especially, where people sleep; their dreams soak into the walls, investing the dwellings with living energy, for good or ill. Have you asked this dwelling if you could enter?"

"No."

"It let you in anyway. It knows you."

"It won't let me leave."

"Have you completed your business here, and asked to exit?"

"No."

He stroked my hair. "If you are determined to leave and a dwelling tries to trap you, you can step sideways into the meadow and then emerge where you choose. But a gentle aspect will take you far. Respect will help you."

"Step sideways?"

"Close your eyes and see the meadow where we were."

I did it.

"Take a step."

I stepped.

"Open your eyes."

We were back in the night-dark meadow where the grass glowed.

He smiled at me. "Now. Find your way back."

I closed my eyes and thought about my parents' front hall. I took a step. I opened my eyes and stared at the coat rack where Dad's fedora hung (he never wore it), Mom's backpack drooped in its straps, and my rain slicker dangled—I had forgotten to take it when I moved out. I turned to thank Hermes, but he was no longer with me.

"Thanks for letting me in," I said to the door. I patted the wood. It felt warmer than it had before. Feeling a little stupid, I went upstairs.

The digital clock on my mom's bedside table said 4:32. Dad's snores were gentle, rhythmic as waves slapping against a dock. I went over to Mom's vanity and sat on the tuffet. The urge to weep washed over me. They might never know where I had gone. If they ever found out—

—an image of my dead self, twisted and horrible—

—it would hurt them even worse. My torture had been finite; theirs might go on for years.

"Mom," I whispered.

My mother's breathing shortened.

"Mom?"

She turned over. "Wha?"

"Mom? Can you hear me?"

She sighed. She rubbed her eyes. She sat up, blew out a breath.

"Mom?"

She took a sip of water from the glass on her bedside table, then lay down, her back to me, and her breath lengthened again.

"Mom," I said, out loud, but there was no response.

I looked at the key I held, a gift from Hermes. I sat a little longer, wondering if this was the right time for its first use.

I didn't know what Steve and his friends did with their

corpses. Maybe they ate them or burned them. Maybe Mom would never know.

I thought of a TV show I saw once about missing children, a segment of "Sixty Minutes," where someone whose child had disappeared said, "You wait. You hope. You cry . . . a river of tears."

I went to my mother and plunged the key into her chest. It slid in easily. I gave it a half-turn, and her spirit sat up, loosed from her body, blinking and looking around. "What?" she said.

"Mom, are you awake?"

"Of course I'm awake, Tessa! What do you think?" She glared at me.

"How do you feel?"

"Startled, I guess. What are you doing home? What time is it?" She glanced over at the bedside table, reached out to switch on the lamp. Her hand went through it. She screamed.

"Mom," I said. I took her spirit hands. They felt more solid than the door had, warm and dry. "Mom. Take it easy."

"Is this a dream?" She looked down, saw her own sleeping form. "Yah!" She was still half inside it, up to the waist. "This had better be a dream!"

I started to cry.

"What is it, baby?" she asked. She rose from her body and hugged me.

"Oh, Mom," I said, leaning into her embrace. I sniffled. Her warmth wrapped me up like a cocoon.

She stroked my back the way she had when I was little and hurt. "What is it?"

"Mom . . . I'm dead."

"Don't be ridiculous," she said in a soothing voice.

"I'm dead, and it doesn't hurt anymore. I wanted you to know that."

"This is a strange dream," she said.

"Please remember it. Write it down when you wake up. Promise?"

"How binding is a promise made in a dream?" she mused.

"Promise?"

"All right," she said.

"This is what you have to write: 'Tess is dead, but she feels good. She's happy. It doesn't hurt.' "

"That's so sappy, Tess, and on a symbolic level it's quite disturbing. Why should I dream that you're dead?"

"Because it's not a dream. Mom, I love you. I have to tell Dad now." I reached around her and turned the key, and she slipped out of my arms and back into her body. Her eyes popped open. She sat up and turned on the light, then looked around the room, looked right through me.

I went to Dad, but before I could unlock him, Mom shook him awake. "Henry, I've just had the strangest dream."

He came instantly awake. "What is it, May?"

"I dreamed that Tess was dead."

"What?"

"Wait a minute, I promised to write it down." She picked up the pen and steno pad she kept on the bedside table, wrote the date: November 1, and, in quotes, "Tess is dead, but she feels good. She's happy. It doesn't hurt." She showed it to Dad.

"What did we have for supper last night?" Dad said. He rubbed his eyes. He yawned. Then he glanced at Mom and the steno pad again. "Hmm." He reached for the phone and dialed my number. The phone rang and rang. "Oh, God," he said faintly. "She's not home."

"Last night was Halloween. Maybe she spent the night at a friend's house."

"May," said Dad. His voice trembled. "Tell me about your dream."

★ ★ ★ ★ ★

They called the police, who refused to get worked up about it. "Let us know when she's been missing twenty-four hours."

They sat in the kitchen, wearing bathrobes and drinking instant coffee. "She didn't say how she died?" Dad asked. He was doodling on Mom's steno pad. "Why? Where?"

"It was just a dream," said Mom.

It was six-thirty a.m. "I'm going to call her next-door neighbor," Dad said, and he did.

Abby wasn't thrilled to wake up so early. I could near her hungover voice from across the room. "Maybe she slept over at some guy's house, didja ever think of that? Don't call this number again, I've already got a splitting headache!" she shrilled, and hung up.

"What guy?" Dad asked into the dead phone.

I didn't know what to do. I could answer all Dad's questions if I used the skeleton key again, but would that be right? The key hadn't come with instructions beyond basic use. Did it hurt people when I used it?

Mom seemed to be okay.

I went to Dad, slipped the key into his back, turned it. His body slumped, his cheek hitting the table, and the phone slipped from his hand. His spirit, still sitting up straight, looked around, startled but alert. "Tess," he said. "What am I making all this fuss about when you're right here?" He glanced down at the back of his body's head. "Yow!" he said. He reached out and his hand passed through his own head. "What! Am I awake? How can this be?"

"It's the only way I can talk to you, Daddy," I said.

"What?"

"Henry? Henry?" Mom was shaking Dad's body. "What happened? Are you all right?" She felt for his pulse.

I gripped Dad's hand and pulled him out of himself to get him away from the action. "I'll talk fast and then I'll put you back inside, Dad. I'm dead. I'm a ghost. The way I died was horrible. That's why I wanted to let you know I'm okay now."

"How can you be okay when you're dead?"

A little strangled laugh rose in my throat. "I know it sounds weird. I have a friend over here who helped me. I just didn't want you thinking . . ."

"Thinking what?"

"I don't know. Whatever. That you ever did anything wrong, or that there was anything you could have done to save me or help me. You are a great father. I love you. And I'm okay."

"Tessie . . ."

"I don't know if they're going to find me. If they do, it's going to be really, really awful for you. Just remember. I'm all right now." I hugged him and led him back to his body. Mom was really getting upset now.

"Where are you?" Dad asked me. He tried to watch me, but he kept getting distracted by Mom's efforts to revive his body.

"I'm here."

"I mean, where's your body?" he asked as I reached for the key.

"The last time I saw it, it was in an abandoned church."

"When did you die?"

"Sometime last night."

"Okay." He patted my cheek. "Okay."

I kissed him and turned the key.

He sat up.

"What happened?" Mom asked. "Are you all right?"

"Just a little out-of-body experience. I was talking to Tess. Oh, May. I think she really is dead." He made notes: abandoned church, Halloween night. "Oh," he said, staring at his notes. "Oh." His face paled. "It's the Satanists."

Mom stared at him a moment, her eyes wide. Then she went to the sink and threw up.

For the first time I remembered that they had killed somebody last Halloween, too. Not here in Holdfield, but in Mostyn, a little town six miles south. A girl named Deedee Christy, sixteen; the police had withheld most of the details, but the stories going around were so gross I got sick just thinking about them, and I had put them out of my mind.

Last Halloween, this Halloween—what about next Halloween?

Mom rinsed out her mouth with water, gargled, spat in the sink. "She's happy. It feels good. She's safe," she said. "Oh, Henry . . ."

"Tess, are you here?" Dad asked in a low voice.

"Yes," I said, but he couldn't hear me.

He sighed. "Tess, when I was just talking to you, you—you said something about putting me back inside. Does that mean you can take me out again? What is that? If you can do it, please do it again, all right?" And then, in an aside to Mom, "If I slump again, don't worry. I think she's doing it." He moved his coffee cup and the steno pad out of his way and laid his head and arms on the table.

I slid the skeleton key into his back and turned it, and he came loose again, rose to his feet, staring at me. His body sagged. Mom looked this way and that. He glanced back at her, then down at himself, finally again at me.

"Was it the Satanists, Tess?"

"Yes," I said.

"Tess," said Mom, "let me talk to you too." She leaned against the table the way Dad had, like a little kid taking a nap at her desk. I pulled the key out of Dad without relocking it and slid it into Mom, turning it. She rose up, looked at herself and Dad doubled. "Oh," she muttered, and touched her mouth with her fingers.

"How did you do that?" Dad said. He reached for Mom's body, but his hand went through the key, and through Mom, too.

"It was a gift," I said.

"This is going to sound really stupid," Dad said. "Are you a minion of Satan now?" Then, in a mutter to himself, "Minion? Is that the technical term?"

I laughed and said, "No, Dad. I cheated them, because I had my own god. I don't think they got much good out of killing me."

"Your own god?" said Dad, astonished.

"Hermes," said Mom at the same time.

"I told him I wasn't ready to take the next step yet, and he said I can stay here for a while if I need to. I didn't want you to . . . find out the hard way about me."

Mom came and hugged me. It felt just like a real hug, a hard one, flesh and bones, breath and beating heart to beating heart. I kept my arms around her too, despair and crushed hope and love lodged in my chest like an arrowhead, burning and yet pleasant. Dad came and put his arms around both of us. I felt like I had when I was ten and really totaled my bike, skinned and scraped myself, bit my lip. I had thought maybe if we all hugged hard enough the pain would go away. And in a weird way it had worked.

"Hermes," said Dad when at length we all let go of each other. "How do you worship this guy?"

Sasha came to my funeral.

So did Steve.

By that time I had worked with some of my other gifts,

27

enough to be able to hold a pencil (if the pencil would let me) or to move matter (if the matter was agreeable, and a surprising lot of it was, when approached politely). When Mom and Dad were going through my apartment, I wrote them notes about what to do with my possessions. Unlocking Mom and Dad and then putting them back would have taken too long.

We developed a whole lot of shortcuts. Mom carried her steno pad everywhere, holding a blank page up occasionally to give me the opportunity to tell her something. The pencil was tied to a string, which was fastened to the spiral binding. It soon got used to me.

My parents took my altar to Hermes and set it up on the mantel at home. With every meal they made an offering to him.

Mom let someone else on the paper handle the story of my death. She took a leave of absence from the paper, and everyone understood. Again, the police withheld a lot of the details, but everyone knew Mom and Dad had gone in to identify the body, which was found where I had left it, within a circle of black candle stumps in an old desecrated church.

Sasha arrived at my parents' house before the funeral, enveloped in a green cape, the scent of autumn leaves hanging around her like perfume. Her auburn hair hung lusterless to her shoulders, and her hazel eyes looked too large in her face. She had lost weight since I saw her in August. She looked tense and nervous. "I'm so terribly sorry, Mr. and Mrs. Hector," she said, standing on the front porch, her hands buried in her pockets, her shoulders hunched.

"Come in, come in," Mom said, putting an arm around Sasha's shoulders and wafting her into the house.

"Tess will be so glad you're here," said Dad.

Sasha paled as Mom closed the door behind her. She

looked around the front hall as if searching out a fast exit.

I tugged on Dad's sleeve. "Oh," he said. "Wrong thing to say, eh? Sorry, Sasha. I'm getting a little absent-minded lately."

"That's quite all right," she said in a thin voice.

"We're glad you could make it, Sasha," said Mom. Sasha glanced at her sharply. I thought Mom sounded a little too cheerful for a funeral too. More like she had just gotten a positive R.S.V.P. for a birthday party.

But then, everybody thought my parents were much too chirpy for having lost their daughter in such an ugly way.

"You're more than welcome to stay here," Dad said.

Sasha wavered, then said, "I'd like that."

"Good. Good," said Dad. "Would you like tea or cocoa? You look chilled."

"I do feel cold."

"Come into the kitchen."

When they had her sitting between them at the kitchen table with a mug of cocoa warming her hands and her cape half off, Mom said, "Sasha, we do need to tell you about Tess. When you're ready."

"What is there to tell?"

"There are some things she wanted you to know," Dad said.

"Did she leave me a letter?"

"Kind of," said Mom.

"Is it private?"

"She told us, too."

Sasha sipped cocoa, looking back and forth between my mom and my dad. She had never spent much time at my house. Her parents had a big screen TV and an air corn popper, so we had watched movies at her house. The rest of the time we were out in the weather, or sneaking off someplace, or searching out obscure Greekisms in the library. "I think," she said. "I think I'm ready."

Mom picked up the steno pad. "Faith is rewarding," she read.

Sasha frowned. "Did Tess find Jesus before she died?" she said, then gasped. "Oh! I'm sorry, I'm sorry!"

"Why?" asked Dad.

"Because of the way—"

"Oh." He thought for a second. "That would be ironic, wouldn't it? She finds Jesus and dies at the hands of Satanists?"

"How can you say that?" Sasha asked, shocked.

"Because you could think it. It's all right, Sasha. We're not nuts. Really we aren't. And we're not denying what happened. We . . ."

"We've had a lot of help," said Mom. "Sasha, Tess wants you to know that faith in Hermes is justified."

Sasha's mug banged down on the table top. The color drained out of her face. "No," she said, "no. I'm getting out of here." She stood up.

"What are you afraid of?" Dad asked.

"Tess would never tell you any of this! The Sisterhood was secret. What have you done? Gone through all her private things, like ghouls?"

"We did whatever Tess asked us to," Mom said. "But I do think if my daughter was dead and I didn't know how she would have wished her things disposed of, I really think it would be all right for me to read whatever record she left behind. I think that would be a parent's prerogative."

"We didn't have to do that, because her ghost is here," said Dad.

"Oh, no," said Sasha, shaking her head. "No. You're

gone. Right around the bend."

I grabbed my friend the pencil and wrote to Mom, "Ask her if that's the technical psychological term for this."

Mom sat back with her arms crossed while I wrote, and when I was finished, she flicked her eyebrows at Sasha, who had been watching the pencil move. Sasha, her hands trembling, leaned over far enough to read the message. She licked her lips. "No," she said. "I don't know what the DSM-III-R diagnosis would be for this. Severe psycho-social stressors on one of the axes, I bet." Then she sort of fell back into her chair. "Tess?" she whispered.

"Yes," I wrote.

"It's your handwriting. Is it really you?"

"Yes," I wrote. "I'm a wandering shade. I wanted to wander over to where you are, but I don't know much about traveling yet, especially to someplace I've never been. I'm so glad you came, Sasha."

She reached out and touched the paper, tracing the letters of her name with her fingertip. She shivered. Then she looked up at Mom and Dad.

"If you actually want to *see* her, to talk with her, she can unlock your spirit from your body, and then it's like she's standing in front of you," Dad said. "If you're prepared to risk it."

She thought about that for a while. She took a sip of cocoa, licked chocolate off her lip. She touched my writing again. "Does it hurt?"

"No," said Mom. "Unless you're not braced for it. Then you can bruise yourself."

"How do I brace for it?"

Mom showed her how to lay her head and arms on the table top. With her cheek pressed to the Formica, Sasha said, "Okay. I'm ready."

I unlocked her. She sat up and looked around. "Tess," she whispered.

I held out my hands to her and she took them. I pulled her free. "Oh, Tess," she said, and hugged me.

"It was a nightmare," she said a little later, "reading about it."

"He came and rescued me, Sasha."

"He?"

"Hermes," I said, and then he stood beside me and smiled down at Sasha.

"Oh my god," she said, and he laughed.

"This is what I wanted you to know. It's real," I said.

"Oh my god."

"I hear your prayers, even when there is no faith behind them," he said. "The mere act of praying generates faith."

"Oh my god."

"A short prayer, but a useful one." He touched Sasha's head. "I am glad you found me, priestess." He vanished.

"Tess!" Sasha wailed.

"It's okay, Sasha. Really it is. When you have time to think about this . . ." I shook my head. I didn't know what she would think. "Listen, I should put you back now. If you stay out too long your body has trouble breathing. I just wanted you to know I'm still here for a while—until I feel ready to go on—so if you want to talk, just tell me. I can do that pencil thing, or I can unlock you. I can hear you. If I'm near, anyway."

She touched my face. She stroked my hair. She looked behind her at the table, where Mom and Dad sat beside her still form, sipping their own cocoa and not saying anything. "Tess . . ."

"Yes?"

"Don't you hate those people for hurting you?"

"Yes," I said. "That's one of the things keeping me here. I guess I'm not supposed to hate them, but I do. I want them hurt. He says it'll wear off, but I haven't lost it yet."

"Oh," she said. She sighed and went to stand by her body. I relocked her spirit inside her. She took a few deep breaths and sat up. Then she sat there shaking her head and looking at my parents, who smiled at her.

"Feel better?" Mom asked.

Sasha changed her shake to a nod. She bit her lower lip. "I feel—" Trembling took her over. She sat in the chair and shook for a while. Mom patted her shoulder and waited it out.

"Was this hard for you?" Sasha asked them at last.

"It would have been much worse if she hadn't come back," said Dad.

"I've been playing with this belief for five years," Sasha said. "I thought it was just a game. But I just met my god." She got up and started pacing around. "People aren't supposed to be able to *meet* their gods; that's the point of gods, they're just ideas off in the mist somewhere and people use god-ideas to control their own behavior or excuse it or something, but . . ." She paced and paced. "First I meet a *ghost*, and then I meet a *god* I thought I made up—"

"Rough day," said Dad. "Maybe you need to lie down?"

"Yes," said Sasha. "Yes."

"Will you be okay in Tess's old room?"

"Yes," said Sasha, with a huge sigh.

I wasn't paying much attention to my memorial service. I was looking at the flowers banked around my closed casket, moving the cards just enough to read them, and I was looking at members of my extended family whom I hadn't seen since the family Fourth of July picnic last summer, aunts and uncles and cousins all dressed in dark colors and looking sad;

and sometimes I watched Mom and Dad and Sasha in the front pew. Sasha sat next to Dad; Dad sat next to Mom; Mom sat next to Flo Reitz, a friend from the newspaper, somebody I'd called Aunt Flo since I was six, who was covering the funeral for the paper—who had, in fact, been covering the whole story of my murder.

The steno pad lay between Sasha and the pew's edge, shielded from casual view by her skirt and the flare of the pew's end.

I felt strange and sad, and wondered how everybody was doing. My cousin Marisha was actually crying. I had never seen her cry before. My dad's brother, Uncle Jake, had reddened eyes; he was holding tight to Aunt Mary's hand. Well, sure, I had always liked him too. He had taught me chess, and I had spent most of my twelfth summer at his house with my cousins Amy, Bert, and Lucy.

Feeling like I was peeping at private grief, I walked farther back, wondering who all these people were; I didn't know half of them. Friends of Mom's and Dad's from work, I decided after some study.

Steve slipped in about halfway through the service.

I couldn't believe it.

He had a black suit on, and a black bolo tie with a silver scorpion clasp; and even though one of the ushers tried to direct him to a seat, he stood in back, his arms crossed over his chest, and just listened.

I stared at his face, but he wasn't wearing an expression. I wondered what he felt. Had he gotten satisfaction out of what he had done to me? Did Satan let his followers know when he was pleased with them? Or displeased with them? After my encounters with my own god, I wasn't sure what anybody else's did for them.

Steve frowned.

I remembered who I was and where. I glanced down at myself. Since my death I had been wearing the simple white bridal dress Steve had given me Halloween night, though without the stains and rips it had acquired in the course of that night. I held out my hands and my fingers curled into fists. Rage ignited inside me, flaring high until I felt as if anything I touched would burst into flame. How dare he! How dare he take me when I trusted him, take me and hurt me and kill me? How dare he come here after having done that?

I found myself beside the front pew. I reached through the wood, gripped the pencil, and wrote, "He's here. At the back of the church. The man who killed me." I threw the pencil down. It bounced once and then rolled off the pew.

Mom, Dad, Sasha glanced over. Flo glanced over. Sasha's eyes widened as she read what I had written. Then she pressed the steno pad to her breast, hiding it from Flo. She gave a little nervous smile and bent to retrieve the pencil. Flo faced front again. Sasha handed the pad to Dad, who gave Mom a glimpse of it. All three of them turned to look back at Steve.

After a moment he felt their regard and stared back at them. His eyes were ice-cold. How had I ever found him friendly? Danger was like a black shroud around him, edged with silver.

Dad half rose. I tugged on his sleeve. "We can't let him get away," he whispered.

Steve was smiling now. My anger was freezing into fear. Steve could still hurt me by hurting Dad or Mom. They were forewarned—but Steve had lots of friends, some of them possibly augmented by their faith. I pulled Dad's sleeve hard. He sat down again, muttering, "What? What?"

"Henry, are you all right?" Flo asked.

Above us, the priest was still talking about his god and my

life. Dad looked around, then said, "Flo, the murderer is standing in the back of the church. I want to stop him before he gets away."

Flo glanced back at Steve, who smiled at her, too. "My god," she said. She swallowed. "How do you know? The police haven't been able to find anything solid."

"Trust me on this."

"I'll go call the cops." She slipped out the end of the pew, and slid soundlessly down the side aisle toward the back. Dad kept his eye on Steve.

Steve moved over and blocked Flo's exit, catching her wrist. But by this time some of the other people had noticed Dad constantly looking back, and they turned too, to see Steve hanging onto Flo as she tried to twist free.

The priest paused. "Young man?" he said, which I thought took guts, since the priest looked barely older than Steve, and much less effective.

Steve smiled.

"Is there a problem? You're disturbing our service."

"I'm sorry. I came to the wrong place," said Steve. "I was looking for the funeral of a girl who died in service to God. Come on, Ma." Keeping his grip on Flo's wrist, he pulled her out of the door.

Mom stood up. Dad started to his feet again. Before he had gotten very far, I unlocked him. His body sagged back down in the pew. Sasha stared at him, then looked around as if searching for a shadow. "Dad, stay here—" I said. "I'll follow them. Don't let him get you, too."

"Tell me what happens, tell me where they go, Tess—oh, Tess—"

"He's dangerous, Dad. Stay here." I locked him in and fled after Steve and Flo.

Who hadn't gotten very far. Flo was yelling, gripping the

arm of one of the solemn young men who drifted around the corridors in the funeral home. "Help me," she said, "help me, this man is a murderer."

"Up to your old tricks, Ma?" said Steve. He smiled at the young man. "She has these psychotic episodes. The doctor cautioned me against restimulating her with this funeral, but I just thought—such a close member of the family—she ought to have a chance to say goodbye. I think I'd better get her back to Reston. Come on, Ma." He pulled her fingers off the young man's arm one at a time.

"Help me," Flo said. "This man murdered Tess Hector."

Steve still smiled. I remembered that smile. It was his most irresistible one, the one that insisted we were in a conspiracy together, and wasn't it fun? He was using it full power on the young man.

"I'm Florence Reitz, with the *Holdfield Guardian*, and this man is trying to silence me," said Flo. "Call the police!"

The young man looked bewildered. He opened his mouth.

"I appeal to you as one human being to another," Flo said in a low voice. "Help me. Help me." She kicked at Steve's crotch.

"Now, now, Ma," said Steve, pinching her shoulder. She grimaced.

"I—" said the young man. Steve smiled at him again and jerked Flo out of the building.

"You've got a good spirit in you," Steve said to Flo, dragging her toward his car, a black mid-seventies Mustang. "I like that."

Flo screamed. She struck him in the face with her free hand, and kicked at him. He pinched her shoulder again and she wilted.

I thrust the skeleton key into Steve's chest and turned it, and his body tumbled to the concrete sidewalk. Flo broke its grip on her and fled.

Steve's spirit stood before me. He was tall and pale and starved-looking. I could see through him. On the inside of his spirit skin there were a million wounds and scabs, some old and crusty, some fresh and bleeding. As I watched, he reached inside himself and picked at the scab over his heart, pulled it until fresh blood flowed. Then he stared at his reddened fingers with their rosy halo of spirit blood. At length he looked up at me.

"Tess," he said. He stared at me from my bare toes to the curly hair on my head. "What are you doing still here? This is why the Master was angry? Because you never crossed over?" He raked his fingernails across his stomach, swiping right and left, opening fresh wounds.

"You can't spend what I've already donated," I said. I searched myself for the rage that had fueled me in the church, but it was gone now, replaced by a creeping horror at what Steve was doing to himself.

"You have broken my communion with my god by being an imperfect sacrifice," Steve said, and pulled off a great scab in his head. "I will never regain his trust. I worked so hard, so long to get where I was—"

He flickered. For a moment I saw a little boy in his place, small, frightened, wounded, cupping his hands over his genitals and looking up with huge eyes for the direction of the next bruising blow. Inside him there flared a white light, which dimmed immediately.

"—and you destroyed everything!" And then he was lunging at me, reaching for me with his dripping red hands.

I closed my eyes and stepped into the midnight meadow, where I trembled and looked all around to see if Steve had somehow followed me. But I was alone.

"Hermes," I whispered, and my god came to me, stepping

out of the air. "I'm frightened," I said.

He hugged me. After a little while, he whispered, "You are under my protection. He cannot harm you anymore."

"I didn't know if you knew what was happening."

"I learned."

I leaned my head against his chest, absorbing his support. Then I pushed away a little. "All right," I said. "I'll go back."

"Here," he said, handing me his *caduceus*.

Wordless, I gripped it. It was lighter than it looked, the twined serpents somehow balancing it so that its weight lay in some other plane.

He laid his palm on my forehead. I felt warmth enter me from it, melting into me like sunlight.

"Thank you," I said. I closed my eyes, thinking of the sidewalk in front of the funeral home, and took a step.

Steve's shade was plucking at his body, trying to slip back inside. The body's breathing was laboring and ragged. Dad, Mom, Sasha, and Flo stood around it. I could hear approaching sirens, still distant.

"Tess," said Sasha, urgently. "Tess, where are you?"

I went to Steve. His spirit looked up at me. "Are you trying to kill me?" he said.

"Turnabout," I began, but the *caduceus* stirred in my hand. I stared at the snakes on it and they stared back. "Steve," I said, and held the wand out. Golden light flowed from it, washing down over Steve; under that gentle flood, his sores and scabs washed away, leaving his skin clean and whole.

"No!" he screamed. "No, you're destroying my identity!"

I lifted the *caduceus*, cutting off the flow of healing. "You *like* what you are?"

"This is who I am," he said. He scratched a new bloody

39

furrow across the inside of his chest. "If you change it, I'll lose myself."

"But—" I remembered the clear white light inside the little boy, and looked for it. Inside Steve there was only darkness. Except the little boy had been inside Steve, too . . . "But—I can't wait any longer," I said, and leaned down to twist the key in his chest and lock him back in his body.

The body's breathing strengthened. Presently Steve opened his eyes, looking up at the people around him.

"Just lie still, son," said Dad. "Help is coming."

"Are you crazy?" Steve asked, his voice raw. He tried to get up, but he'd been away too long.

"Probably I am," said Dad. An ambulance and a police car pulled up simultaneously. Steve struggled to get up again, and again he failed. Dad knelt beside him. "Why did you do it?" he whispered to Steve. "Why did you kill my daughter?"

"My god wants blood," Steve muttered. "My blood isn't good enough. My god wants me to prove I love him. When I give him the perfect sacrifice, that's when he'll love me back." He frowned then, and glared at Dad, as if he was angry because Dad had made him say something.

Dad touched Steve's hand. Then the ambulance guys were shooing everybody away so they could take Steve's pulse and blood pressure and lift him onto a stretcher.

"Your daughter couldn't even die right," Steve yelled as they put him in the ambulance.

Sasha drove me to the university and showed me her room. With my help, she set up an altar to Hermes in a desk drawer, where she could lock it when she was gone, and unveil it when she was home. Once I had seen what her place looked like, I could step out of the meadow to there anytime. She put a steno pad and a pencil on her desk so I could leave her notes.

Mom and Dad went to grief counseling, and to a special counselor who worked with the victims of violent crimes and their families. Sometimes Mom told me about the sessions, but more often not.

I spent a lot of my time walking the streets of Holdfield, passing through buildings if they admitted me, staring into people's faces. I found five more of the people who had been in the circle the night of my death. One was a sales clerk at the perfume counter of a department store. One was a short order cook at a burger place. One was a doctor. One worked at a day care center. One was a mechanic in a garage for foreign cars.

I followed two of them home, and their houses were soaked with pain dreams and wouldn't let me in.

One day I was walking down a street and realized that my feet refused to touch the ground; I was floating a yard above the sidewalk. I was losing touch.

It was time to go on.

Objects of Desire

Everyone was getting skewlis. I wanted one so much it hurt.

I didn't know about trends. I hated that when three of my friends got black high-top shoes with light-up lightning bolts on them, I wanted my own pair *sooo* much. I mean, why should I care? It was like some chip in my head switched on and said WANT. It kept digging at me until I whined at Mom.

She used to just give me whatever I wanted, but since her job diminishment, she couldn't afford to do that anymore.

Sometimes she talked to me about worldview, global perspective, how we were small in something giant and we had to work with all the other things to get along okay, and when I listened hard enough, I could shut the WANT chip off.

Sometimes she just said, "Kirby, shut up about it now," but the chip kept sending the WANT message. It was hard to ignore.

So anyway, people at school started showing up with skewlis. Sort of a cross between a weasel and a cat: skewlis had round heads with cute pointy ears and big eyes, slinky arms and legs that wrapped around your arm, and long bodies that bent when your elbow bent. They came in designer colors and patterns like Blue Razzberry and Circuitboard and Seawave. Smart enough to fetch, open cupboards and drawers, learn cute tricks, and accomplish small tasks. Motivated by specially engineered snacks that kept them willing and docile. Guaranteed by the F.P.A. to not be usable as weapons.

Pretty soon most of my friends and a lot of other kids were walking around with skewlis heads on one shoulder or the other, skewlis bodies doubling the width of one arm. People looked like mutants. Honto cool mutants.

The best skewlis brands had tons of max-excellent options. You could computer-blend a color scheme and the company would build you a skewlis to match. You could pick traits like "makes musical noises" or "will act as alarm clock." My friend Pati got one that would hold her bookscreen for her while she read, and press the text-scroll icon when she nodded.

I didn't want a skewlis at first. They were just too weird and creepy.

But after almost everybody I knew got one, I started feeling odd without that extra head on one shoulder, that widening of one arm, that pair of jewel eyes watching every-thing. I felt deformed.

So when Grandma got me a skewlis for my birthday, I was glad.

My fourteenth birthday party was nothing like my thir-teenth birthday party had been. Between this year and last year, Mom lost her big job and had to take little ones, so I couldn't have a huge party and invite tons of friends over.

Mom, Grandma, and I sat around the kitchen table. Mom had managed to get enough meat for us to have my favorite, beef stew, and Grandma had baked me a small square cake and covered it with strawberry frosting. Which was a great switch from basic rations. No matter what color or shape they make base, it all tastes pretty much like cardboard.

After we ate dinner and the cake and said how great it tasted, I opened my two presents: a new pen with temperature-sensitive skin that changed colors, and a silver shirt with a hologram of my favorite band on the front. Both of these presents were things I really liked. I throttled the little voice inside that whined because I didn't get more. I said a lot of thank-yous and hugged my presents and figured that was it.

Then Grandma brought the carry-cage out from under the table. A faint smell of lemons and incense came from the cage.

She set the carry-cage in front of me.

For a second I couldn't breathe. I knew we couldn't afford what I really wanted. Maybe she had gotten me a kitten. That would be okay. If Mom said it was, anyway. I would need to get extra after-school jobs so I could buy cat food.

I leaned forward and opened the door of the ribbon-wound carry-cage.

The skewlis emerged slowly. At first I thought it was gray, and I felt a flicker of disappointment. At school, people fussed most about skewlis with bright colors: turquoise, cotton-candy pink, acid green with baby-blue stripes. This one looked dull in comparison.

Then light glanced off it, and I saw that it was a soft lavender color. Its huge eyes glowed orange-red. Its front feet looked just like little black hands. It came out onto the table among the confetti and torn gift wrapping, then sat back and stared up at me.

I stared back, wondering what it was thinking. What did any pet think confronted with a new owner? *I have to spend the rest of my life with you whether I like it or not? Amuse me? Oh, no?*

It lifted one small black hand and held it palm outward toward me. Confused, I lifted my own hand in answer and slowly brought it forward.

The skewlis touched its palm to mine. Its hand felt hard and small and hot. My hand tingled around its touch. It made a chirring noise, jumped over my hand, and clamped its arms

44

around my upper arm, bringing its head up beside mine. Its lemony smell grew stronger for a second, then faded. The tip of a pink tongue flicked from its mouth. Its orange eyes stared at my face from unnervingly close.

It seemed to weigh almost nothing. The grip of its arms and legs around my arm felt weird for a moment, but then I stopped noticing. I turned to Grandma. "Thank you," I whispered. "Thank you."

"Oh, good," she said. "I hoped you would like it." She hesitated, then said, "It's not one of the famous brands."

Grandma was a veteran bargain hunter. She specialized in factory seconds, reconditioned obsolescence, open box returns, and "that stain is so small no one else will ever notice it, but they knocked five dollars off anyway." I used to think she was funny and irritating about that stuff, but lately I'd been trying to learn how she did it.

The best skewlis on the market had small seven-pointed stars branded onto their hind legs. There were two other acceptable brands, but after that, you got into the gray area of copycat skewlis. Rip-off companies put together inferior versions. I'd heard about near-skewlis fakes and their problems.

I didn't want to think about that on my birthday, when my grandmother had just given me the perfect present.

My skewlis had a brand I'd never seen before, a little blue spiral almost hidden by the silver-lavender fur on its hind leg.

"It's all right," I said.

"It doesn't have any of those fancy features," she continued, looking worried.

"It's great, Grandma," I said. "It's perfect. Thank you." With the skewlis so close to me now, I could see a very faint tiger-stripe pattern in blue over the silvery lavender of its coat. My skewlis looked like a ghost version of others I had seen, and I thought it was really honto neat.

"What will you call him, Kirby?" Mom asked me. Her voice had a familiar edge to it. Grandma had done something important without asking her again. Mom was mad. But it was my birthday, and she didn't want to be the bad guy.

I stroked my finger over the top of the skewlis's head. It closed its eyes and chirred. "Her name is Vespa," I said in a small voice.

Vespa opened her eyes to stare into mine. Her chirrs grew louder. I didn't remember any of my friends' skewlis making noises like this, but it sure made me feel warm and strange.

"Vespa?" Mom said. "You're naming her after a scooter?"

"Huh? I don't know what you mean. It's just her name."

"Oh," she said. She smiled and shook her head.

I looked at Grandma. "Is there a manual? How do I take care of her? What do I feed her?" I thought about the special food my friends fed their skewlis: small soft brown cubes. I wondered how expensive it was. Probably really expensive, the way most designer stuff was. Had Grandma bought some? Was Vespa hungry now?

Grandma licked her lips, looking away from Mom's accusing stare. "There's no manual," she said. "The man I got her from told me she'll eat what humans eat, and she just needs a little box with sand in the bottom to do her duties in. Always give her access to fresh water, and bathe her about once a week with water and baby shampoo. He said . . . he said she'll teach you what she needs." She reached under the table and brought up a small sack of cat litter and a high-sided plastic tray. "For starters," she said.

"Thanks!"

Vespa rubbed her head against the side of my head. Her fur was exquisitely soft. She smelled so good. Lemon, stick incense, fresh bread.

There wasn't much left of dinner, it had all been so good. I pressed cake crumbs together and held them up in my hand. Vespa reached out, grabbed a handful, and sniffed them, then ate them. She chirped.

"You can keep the carry-cage," Grandma said.

"Thank you, Grandma. It's a terrific present. Thank you." I glanced at Mom. "I'll get more babysitting jobs. I'll make enough money to feed her," I said. "She's so little, I bet it won't take much."

Mom's frown softened. "Oh, Kirby, it's not that."

Whatever it was, I didn't want to hear about it now. I just wanted to be happy for a little while. "Thanks, everybody, for the best presents and a great meal," I said.

I didn't even have to rack the dishes that night. I took my new things up to my room.

I only thought for a little while about the mountain of presents I had gotten last year when we could afford a big party, when Mom had loved getting me anything I wanted. A lot of those presents were broken and gone now, and a few I had sold so I could get some honto rad school clothes this year instead of the basics that Mom could afford.

I still had my lightning-bolt shoes from last year. Nobody in my class except me wore them anymore, but I still liked them, even though the batteries in the bolts were almost dead and the lightning only flickered when it rained.

It had been kind of weird not following everybody else from one trend to the next since Mom's downgrade. I watched how much I wanted something when all the other kids got it, and I watched how much I didn't want it two or three weeks later when they had moved on to something else. I felt like I was getting this figured out.

Until I got *total* skewlis envy, no matter how hard I tried to pretend I thought they were creepy and weird.

But so what? Grandma had done it! She'd managed to get

a skewlis for me, who knew how! I didn't have to fight my longing anymore.

I glanced at Vespa. Her furry cheek was close to mine. She scanned my bedroom with fire-orange eyes. Warmth spread through me.

What if everybody had already moved on from skewlis to something else? What if, when I got to school tomorrow morning, I was the only one with a skewlis?

Vespa turned and stared into my eyes. I remembered how much I had wanted a skewlis, even though I knew there was no way. This time I didn't want my wanting to fade. I had Vespa. I needed to keep on wanting her, for both our sakes.

She reached out a tiny black hand and patted my cheek. Her fingers were warm. She grasped my earlobe, stared at it, and muttered small sounds more like bird-chirps than purrs. My throat tightened for a moment. I felt amazingly happy.

I filled a cup with water in the bathroom and showed it to Vespa. She jumped down off my shoulder and drank three cups full. I also set up the litter box and showed it to her. She stared at it for a long moment, then looked at me sideways. I wasn't sure what to think. What if she had never used a litter box before? Was she even housebroken?

Oh well, deal with that tomorrow, if I had to.

Vespa jumped up onto my right arm. I patted my left shoulder, and after a moment she crept across my shoulders and locked onto my left arm. I cleaned my teeth and washed my face right-handed, with her still clinging to me. I wondered how we would sleep, or how I'd even change into the mega T-shirt I slept in.

But she responded when I patted the bed: jumped down off my arm and curled up, watching me change into my T-shirt. I went into the closet to hang up my clothes, though, and the instant I was out of her sight she made loud beeping/clicking noises that sounded sort of like a burglar alarm. I ducked back into the room and stared at her.

"Che, che," she scolded, reaching one hand out to me and frowning with her eyebrows. She looked like the ruler of the world.

Did all skewlis act like this? I wished I had documentation. Or that I could go downstairs and log on and look for information. But I didn't want to walk in on Mom and Grandma fighting.

I could ask people at school tomorrow.

I slid under the covers and waved the light out. A second later it lit again. Vespa held her hand out to it. She stared at the light for a moment, then looked at me. Her eyes looked spooky with the light coming from the side; small green moons floated in their centers.

Then she bounded up the bed until she was on the pillow next to my head. She held up her arm and waved the "lights-out" signal, and my room darkened.

I listened to her breathing, smelled her lemon-and-fresh-bread scent. I felt keyed up. I couldn't remember how smart my friends' skewlis had been. Could a skewlis figure out complicated cause-and-effect from just seeing it once? Maybe Vespa had learned that light switch trick somewhere else.

She purred.

I'd heard skewlis make all kinds of noises. I'd never heard one purr before. Before I could consider that, though, I got sleepy. The purring sounded so fine and reassuring. Like, "All's right with the world."

I opened my eyes the next morning and felt Vespa's hands on my forehead. She let go a second later, so I wondered if I had dreamed it.

When I went into the closet to get my school clothes, she

49

followed me in. She clasped her arms and legs around my leg, scolding at me. I wondered if I was going to like close attention in such big doses.

Vespa shared my breakfast bars with me, and took a sip of juice concentrate.

What was I going to do about the litter box situation at school? Maybe somebody would explain it to me.

In the halls before school started, skewlis were still everywhere. My friend Pati rushed up to me and complimented me on Vespa. I looked at her baby-blue-eyed, pink-and-green-checked skewlis (named Ramtha) and realized I liked Vespa's coloring much better. Not that I said anything about it. Other friends gathered around and stared at Vespa, checked her brand, nodded to me as if I'd managed to squeak into their club.

I noticed five or six kids in the hall with black buttons big as hands on their jackets. Colored letters, kana, and Sanskrit flashed across the buttons, not making words, just pulling at my eyes.

"Oooo," said Pati, and raced off to inspect one of the buttons.

I noticed the kids with buttons didn't have skewlis. *Well. The Next Hot Thing is here,* I thought.

Vespa patted my forehead. I didn't remember other skewlis doing that to anybody.

But it was strange. The WANT chip had switched on in my brain as soon as Pati ran away to look at buttons, even though I thought I had killed that chip by getting Vespa. I mean, I really thought I had killed that damned chip. What could be better than Vespa?

Stupid black buttons that didn't even make words?

I saw Rico smile as two girls asked him about his flashing button.

Vespa patted my forehead.

And the WANT chip switched off.

It was just school, and I hadn't done all my homework yet because I had celebrated my birthday by not making myself do the subjects I hated. I ignored the bright new buttons and plowed past everybody to get to study hall.

After school Pati and Arco and I walked through the downtown maximall, window-shopping. Pati and Arco went into Everything Matters to look for belts. I didn't go inside. I love that store so much. I always see stuff I want, want, want and can't afford. It's easier for me to just stay out of it and not know what I'm missing. So I wandered over and looked at the food court instead, which was also not a good idea. Vespa and I had shared three lunch bars, and I wasn't hungry at all. But I saw a creampuff with chocolate on top. WANT.

Vespa patted my forehead.

Unwant.

Even though I could almost taste that creamy filling, the nice flaky, buttery pastry texture, the cold, hard bittersweet chocolate shell . . .

Vespa patted my forehead again, and I stopped craving.

Dazed, I wandered into Everything Matters. Glass earrings with little eyeballs in them. Pendants made of splattersteel, jingling and throwing off light. Shoe gewgaws with colored gems all over them. The latest in cutaway gloves. Dice chains, fake eyebrow and nose piercings, and a whole row of wide leather belts with small copper and steel shapes grommeted to them.

WANT.

Pat, pat. Unwant.

"Look," Pati cried, showing me a belt. Gold weave with green gems.

"Pretty," I said as she twisted it around her waist. Her skewlis clung to her arm, but didn't seem to be paying attention.

"No, really," Pati said. "Do you think it's me?"

"It's *so* you," Arco said. "*Ja?* What about this?" She held up a scarf with concentric black and red circles on it, then twisted it around her orange-streaked blonde hair. "*Moi?*" Her butter-yellow, tiger-striped skewlis seemed passive too.

"Def," Pati said.

Last time I had come in here with Pati and Arco and a couple other girls I had been so jealous of their credit ratings I couldn't think straight.

I narrowed my eyes and studied Arco. "Not," I said. "*So* not."

"Honto?" Arco said.

"Too down," I said. It did darken her whole look. "You're an up girl."

"Huh," said Arco. She put the scarf back.

She and Pati experimented with other things in the store. I watched, feeling Vespa's hand on my forehead every once in a while, almost before I knew I was getting sick with wanting again. The want kept going away. I felt a little dizzy and strangely good.

I went outside and over to the window of the leather store. There was a baby-blue suede jacket I had been craving for two weeks. I stared at it and felt nothing, even though Vespa didn't touch my forehead.

I had to sit down.

What was my skewlis doing to me?

I glanced at her. Her head turned as she watched people go by. She seemed fascinated by everything.

I watched too. Lots of people had skewlis grafted to their arms. Most of the skewlis looked tranced or dazed or asleep.

52

None of them patted their people's foreheads. They just looked like . . . accessories.

"What are you?" I whispered to Vespa.

Her orange eyes stared into mine for a long moment.

Then Pati and Arco came out of the store, loaded down with plastic shimmer bags full of stuff. "Let's get pastry!" Arco said, and we went to the food court.

Pati treated me. She'd been doing that since Mom's diminishment. She never said anything about it. She was a good friend.

I gave Vespa a chunk of my brownie.

"Ack!" Pati said. "You're not supposed to do that!"

"Huh?"

"You're never, ever supposed to give them human food," she said. "It kills them."

Vespa ate her piece of brownie in three small neat bites, then licked her delicate black fingers and looked at Pati.

I said, "I didn't get any documentation. Grandma said she was supposed to eat human food. That's all I've fed her, and she hasn't died yet."

Arco shook her head. "That's *so* wrong. First thing in the manual is a great big warning to never feed them anything but their cubes." She broke off a piece of her raspberry doughnut and offered it to her skewlis, who gasped and shook its head. "Yours is weird," Arco said.

I stroked my hand down Vespa's back.

I knew she was weird.

I just didn't know how or why.

"I mean," Pati said. "Not that she isn't neat, or anything." Her face said one thing while her mouth said another.

"I like her a lot," I said.

Both my friends looked glum and uncomfortable.

Oh no, I thought. Not now.

They had stuck by me when Mom diminished. Pati even loaned me stuff that wasn't the latest, but was the next latest, so I wasn't too far behind and people weren't ashamed to be with me. Was my in-ness going to disappear just because my friends thought my pet was strange?

Vespa touched my forehead and I relaxed. Why want? Why fight? It would be all right.

"Eww," said Arco. "It keeps doing that."

"I like it," I said. Though I wasn't sure I did.

Arco's eyes narrowed a fraction. I felt her going away from me. It made me feel dizzy. Like she was on a motorcycle, looking back over her shoulder, and I was standing in the road. I would never catch up again.

I checked Pati to see if she was going away too. She smiled. "Maybe she's the new, improved kind."

I tapped the table with my free hand and Vespa dropped off my arm. She sat on the table in front of me and looked up into my eyes.

"Eww," said Arco. "You let her on the table? That you eat off of?"

"Huh?" There was so much I didn't know about skewlis care. I thought back to the scene in the cafeteria at lunchtime. People still wore their skewlis. In fact, the skewlis acted kind of like clothes, even in gym class. People ate with them on, did track with them on, played tennis and baseball . . . I mean. What was wrong with having them on the table, if they spent so much time on your arm? How different in cootie closeness was that?

I looked around. People at neighboring tables had skewlis. But the skewlis stayed on their arms even as they talked, gestured, used chopsticks or forks or spoons. What was the difference whether the skewlis was on your arm or on the table? I couldn't figure out Arco's distaste. And then I realized.

Nobody else took their skewlis off where you could see it.

I tapped my left shoulder, and Vespa climbed up to lock herself on my left arm.

"She's . . ." Arco said. Her face pinched into a thoughtful frown. "She thinks too much." She shuddered, her yellow skewlis riding it out with flat, uncomprehending eyes.

Vespa blinked and looked down.

The rest of the afternoon she acted like all the other skewlis I could see.

Dumb.

When we got home, though, we could be alone. Mom and Grandma were still out. I sat down in the kitchen where no trace of last night's party remained. I tapped the table, and, after a glance at me, Vespa dropped down.

Grandma and her bargain-sniffing ability. Huh.

"You're not really a skewlis, are you?" I asked.

Vespa wandered across the table, glancing at the salt and pepper shakers. She touched the napkin holder, then paced around the edge of the table and ended up in front of me, exchanging gazes.

Finally she shook her head.

"Not really a skewlis," I said again. "What are you?"

She sat. She patted the table in front of her with one little black hand. Confused, I stared for a minute. Then I put my hand palm up on the table.

She put her hand palm to palm with mine, and I felt a strange tingling again.

Then it was like she talked to me, but not with words, exactly.

You're my test, she told me.

"Your test?"

My . . . experiment. My . . . guinea pig.

I felt totally creeped out then. My skin crawled. The hairs

55

on my arms stood up. Every mad scientist movie I'd ever seen started playing in my head at the same time. "It's alive. ALIVE!"

Vespa tapped my palm. I shuddered and shook my head, then stared at her. She was just some weird little animal, not a mad scientist. Just some kind of computer glitch, probably, a rip-off skewlis whose dealer prep had misfired.

It was hard to believe that when she looked so . . . smart. Perfect. Not wrong.

It had to be something else. But what?

Maybe she was someone's experiment too.

She set her palm to mine again, and I stilled. *You're driven so by want,* she said.

Well, yeah, I thought. Duh.

All of you.

Everyone? It wasn't just me tortured and sliced open by wanting all these things that I usually couldn't get? I thought about Pati racing over to look at someone's shiny button that morning. I bet she knew by now where you could buy those things. She would have her own soon. Then maybe she'd stop wanting.

I was *so* sure. Of course she wouldn't. There would be the Next Hot Thing.

I licked my upper lip. "Okay," I said. "Let me get this straight. You're experimenting on me?" Silly. Idiotic. Scary, even.

She nodded.

"Like, how?" Not that I believed this for a second.

What happens to you when you don't have to want?

Sometimes I made myself sick, wanting things so much.

Today I had walked through Everything Matters, and I'd managed not to want anything in there.

With Vespa patting my forehead, anyway.

Everything in Everything Matters was sooo cool, sooo essential. Yet I didn't actually need any of it.

"What happens to me when I don't have to want?" I wondered out loud.

I don't know yet. Maybe . . .

Before she finished that thought, she snatched her hand out of mine. But I'd seen a swirl of strange pictures and thoughts. Earth from space. The bridge of a spaceship, or close enough, anyway, with lots of small blob-shaped people talking to each other and studying TV programs coming from Earth. An intense fear that these *wanting* people would want so much they would force themselves into space, searching for some elusive thing that wouldn't satisfy them long.

They would boil into space, these Earth people, scorching everything before them and leaving smoke and ash behind.

Unless . . .

Unless they could be taught not to want so fiercely.

Who would they be if that one thing changed?

Why not find out?

"Stay here," I said, jumping up. I ran upstairs to my room and locked the door. Then I wrapped myself in a blanket and curled up in a corner to brood.

Kind of disgusting to think I was just some dumb rat in someone's maze. With, like, electrodes attached to my brain, zap; teach you not to have *that* impulse, zap; run this way, that way, zap. Oops! Ha ha ha, let's get another rat.

Maybe this was just another thing that had happened because of Mom's diminishment. Only people with no money got bargain basement skewlis, which turned out to be alien mad scientists instead.

But Vespa was so much neater than all the other skewlis.

Sure. And she was playing with my mind. Stinging me in my want.

When I didn't really want to want things so much anyway.

Could she make it stop hurting?

But Arco thought it was weird that she patted my head. If she kept doing it, maybe I'd lose all my friends.

Maybe I wouldn't care, because I wouldn't *want* friends.

Ewwwww.

Maybe I'd turn into some kind of robot! Or a walking vegetable. Or just a giant chicken. Buck buck. Or a cow. Chew, chew, chew, moo.

Maybe I'd be happy.

Maybe I'd change into someone else completely.

Would that be so bad?

I thought for a while longer, then wrote myself a note.

DO YOU WANT TO GET OUT OF BED
IN THE MORNING?
IF YOU DON'T, STOP THE EXPERIMENT.

I taped it to the ceiling over my bed, then went downstairs.

Vespa was still sitting on the kitchen table, hugging herself. She looked really worried. Not something I'd ever seen a skewlis do before.

I sat down in front of her, took a deep breath, let it out. "Here's what I want," I said. Then laughed. I started over. "What if this turns me into some kind of walking zombie? I don't want to be a walking zombie! I don't want to be dumber than I already am. I don't want to be a . . . a ghost or an empty person. Do you understand that?"

She nodded.

"I'd kind of like to find out what happens with this experiment too," I said. "But what if it turns out to be a diminishment? I'm scared."

She looked away for a moment, then turned back and nodded.

"If it's just turning me into some stupid goomer, I want you to stop and make it go backward! Can you do that?"

She closed her eyes and hunched her shoulders. She made some little thinking noises. She shifted from side to side.

Then she opened her eyes. She tapped the tabletop with her hand. I put my hand on the table, and she touched my palm.

I can't guarantee I can return you to a pre-change state.

My mind startled up. Oh no. Forget it. Tell her to leave right now. She can find another rat.

It might already be too late for that.

But—huh? I didn't feel changed at all yet. I checked. I was still totally Kirby. As far as I could tell.

I will promise to stop whenever you ask me to, Vespa thought, *and do my best to put wants back inside. You'll still be a little different.*

I took some deep breaths and let them out slowly. This was about the rest of my life. Even if we stopped tomorrow.

After a minute, I said, "Let's do it."

So it's been about a week.

So far what I notice is that it's easier to think. I'm not looking around all the time, distracting myself with thoughts about what I can't have.

I can still rent videos and choose clothes. I still hate green basic rations. I can still think about all the feelings I connect with wanting stuff and not being able to have it. I don't know. It's weird.

Everything happens in tiny pieces. I don't know if I'll know when to stop.

Maybe I won't care.

Unleashed

The baby, Joe, was still nursing when Amelia felt the change coming on, the first stirring of appetite for the forbidden, the faint current of unnatural strength, the hint that she would become the thing she feared and hated. She glanced toward the apartment's living room window. The white curtains were parted, showing that night had arrived as gently as first snow, shadows lodging among the buildings in drifts, melted in spots by the yellow warmth of street lights. She tasted the cool metal of twilight in the autumn air. Soon the moon would crest the hill above town. For the first of its three nights full, the moon would work on her weakly; she could resist change for a little while. But not all night.

Where was the babysitter?

Gently, Amelia pulled Joe free and tucked her breast back into her bra, buttoned her shirt. She rose from the folding metal chair and carried the baby to the closet where she had set up his crib three months before.

Pregnancy had protected her from the moon change, and she had thought nursing would, too. She had prayed that this frightening mother-change in her body would drive out the other, unwelcome change entirely. For a year it had. Just in case, since Joe's birth she had arranged for a babysitter each full moon. Of course, the first time she really needed a sitter, the sitter was late.

Who could she call? She glanced over her shoulder at the phone. The sitter first. Then, maybe, the man who had moved into the apartment downstairs two weeks ago. Amelia usually had trouble talking with strangers, especially men, but something about this man—his smell, perhaps, a musty, stale-sweat-in-body-hair scent that she would have dismissed as unclean, save for its strange attractiveness—had reassured her. They had spoken by the mailboxes three times. He had patted Joe's head with a gentle hand, and Joe had not minded.

What would Mother think of her even considering calling a strange man to look after her child?

Blast that thought. If Mother were alive and knew Amelia had a child at all, she would disown her daughter.

Amelia put Joe in his crib and wound up the music-box mobile above it. By the light of a shell nightlight, plastic cardinals and bluebirds spun to the tune of Brahms' "Lullaby." The baby stared up at the birds. Amelia tucked the blanket in around Joe.

He was such a good baby. Gentle, quiet, undemanding. Just the way she had been as a baby, according to her mother. The way she had been all through girlhood.

She kissed Joe's forehead.

Change gripped her breasts, flattening them against her chest, her body shifting to absorb and redistribute tissue. She backed out of the closet and lay on the rag rug in the tiny living room, her eyes clenched shut, her mind grappling with the change, holding it at bay. When the hunger woke to fullness in her, would Joe be safe?

Kelly Patterson sat on the dirty laundry in his armchair and looked at his apartment. In the two weeks since he had moved in, he had managed to get it as messy as any other place he had lived—crushed beer cans mingling with wadded potato chip bags and filthy socks on the floor, an assortment of dirty shirts and jeans draped across most of the furniture, and a couple crumpled TV dinner trays on the lamp table, right next to the rings left on the wood by wet cans. Sawdust he carried home from the construction site in the cuffs of his pants and in the waffles on his workboots mixed with everything else, but its clean wood scent couldn't compete with the odor of decay, which was almost a color in the air, spiced but not diminished by the scent of soured beer.

By morning it would all be cleaned up and he would have to start over. No matter how much he challenged his animal self, it always rose to the challenge and exceeded it.

Kelly scratched a stubbled cheek. The night Sonya-the-sudden had bitten him—he had forgotten that she had asked him not to come by that night, and he had a record album he was convinced she should hear—the night she had bitten him, he had visualized a lot of scenarios, but never one to match this reality. Who would ever guess that somewhere inside his sloppy self lurked a finicky creature?

Maybe he should stop teasing himself, leave the place neat once and see what his alter ego would do when housekeeping didn't get in its way. Adult-onset lycanthropy. It was still so new and weird. There were lots of experiments he hadn't tried yet. Like, what would he do in the woods? Maybe he should throw a couple blankets, kibble, and a dog dish into the Jeep, drive out into the woods, and check it out—if not tonight, tomorrow. But he had never had any woods sense. What if he got lost? Lost, forty, and naked in the early morning. An ugly thing to contemplate.

He sighed. He stood up and went to the curtains, parted them a crack to check the progress of the night.

There was a thump from upstairs, then a drumming of heels. What was going on with Amelia-the-mouse? Mouse brown hair, mouse dark eyes, alive with the mouse wish to be invisible. Had someone come to visit her, and were they having a go? He had tried to imagine a man who could be the father of her baby, and failed; Amelia was a walking wall of don't-touch-me, though some of the shrug-off softened when he talked to her about the kid. Who could get close enough? Though there was something about her that tempted a person . . .

There was another sharp heel thump on his ceiling, and a low cry that sounded more desperate than satisfied. He straightened out of his habitual slouch, staring up, wondering if she needed someone or something.

The hot silver fire ran through him, starting from his heart and flowing out to his extremities, traveling like flame along gas lines. His fingers tightened on the curtain. He drank a long breath in, feeding the silver fire. Smells sharpened, and sounds intensified; he knew that somewhere in the room was a rat he would soon enjoy catching and eating. He could hear it chewing on leftover pizza in the corner.

A floor away, he could hear Amelia, moaning his name. His first name. Something had to be wrong with her; he couldn't imagine her ever calling somebody male and older than she was by his first name, not under normal circumstances.

He chomped his lip, the pain waking him out of change, dousing the silver fire. It was First Night, the loosest night of change; he could overmaster it, at least for a while. He gripped the knob of his front door.

For a while. What if change caught him in Amelia's place? Scare her out of her skin. She'd get him in trouble, no question.

"Kelly!" she cried.

He opened his door and glanced out. Across the hall, Peter-the-snoop was peeking out. Peter waggled his eyebrows at Kelly and slid his door shut. Kelly sighed and ran for the stairs.

Amelia had the phone's handset in her fist, but she couldn't dial the phone, not with change gripping her. Anyway it was too late. If the sitter hadn't left her building yet, she'd never get here in time.

Soon change would consume Amelia, and she would lose all her normal feelings, her restraints, her cares and concerns. She would go prowling, looking for victims. Before that happened, she must get help for Joe.

Her lower body froze, and the little tail began to grow between her legs. Clenching her fists, locking her elbows, she forced the tail back inside her.

"Kelly!" she cried.

Change whispered through her mind: kill inhibitions. Mate with impulses. Take the night and make it yours. Your feet are made for wandering, and desire is your master.

The doorknob rattled, turned.

She panted short harsh breaths. She could feel her hips slimming, her shoulders changing. Her skin simmered as hair sprouted on chest and arms and legs and back.

Kelly, messy Kelly, slipped into the apartment. " 'Melia?" He knelt beside her.

She unclenched a fist long enough to grip his arm. "Joe," she said, her voice already low and harsh with change. "Will you watch Joe for me?"

"I, uh," he said. His face looked funny, and his smell had changed, though it was still just as enticing. She could feel the racing heat in him against the palm of her hand. "Okay—" he said, on a rising note.

She cried out. All her muscles locked, holding her still while the rest of change happened and she became the monster.

★ ★ ★ ★ ★

It was going to happen. Kelly was going to change in front of somebody for the first time since Sonya had talked him through it. And this time it wasn't going to matter, because—

He wondered who or what had bitten Amelia.

What she was turning into didn't seem to be an animal. Its outline was human.

She shuddered and panted and sweated in front of him, her face twisted in pain and revulsion.

Change didn't hurt him like that. For him, it was as good as sex.

Amelia writhed. He felt he should be watching her, maybe soothing her somehow—a wet towel on the forehead? What?—but his own silver change pulsed through him, and he could no longer hold it off.

Grinning, Adam sat up. Then he glanced down at his lap and frowned. Damn Amelia, the stupid bitch. Why hadn't she changed into his clothes? How could she let him wake up still in a skirt? Didn't she even *care* how he felt? He grabbed handfuls of skirt and ripped it off his body, enjoying the strength in his arms. And this blouse, so obviously feminine, pastel pink, soft and wimpy like the bitch—it had to go too.

Something warm was behind him. He narrowed his eyes. What had happened since last time? He turned and discovered a big black pointy-eared dog standing, staring at him with yellow eyes. Something funny about its paws—they were too big—but before he could get a good look at them, it leaned toward him. An edge of its black lip lifted, showing a long white fang. It made no sound.

"Shoo," he said. His voice wavered.

It took a step toward him.

He stood up, the shreds of skirt scattering around his feet.

He stripped the shirt off and dropped it, then skinned out of Amelia's cotton underpants.

"Didn't know she got a dog," he said to the dog. He wasn't sure how it would behave toward him, either. Did he still smell enough like her to confuse it? He held out a hand to it, and it sniffed him, then backed up one step. "Look, I'll get out," he said. "Just gotta get some clothes first."

The dog sat, its gaze fixed on him.

He went to his closet, the one where she had kept a grudging wardrobe for him. But the clothes were gone. Baby music came from fake birds above a topless cage, and muted light from something orange on the floor. The closet smelled like milk and talcum powder and pee. "Christ!" There was a baby in the cage, a little baby who looked up at him with big eyes. How could she have a baby? A baby in his closet. A baby and a dog! He would have to do something drastic to her. She couldn't keep switching things around on him while he was sleeping. It wasn't fair.

He took a step toward the crib and the big dog growled, low in the back of its throat. He glanced at it. The hair on its spine was standing on end. He shrugged and headed for the bedroom, where he found his clothes in her closet shoved over against the wall, crowded out by her own. Dumb bitch. She'd wrinkled his favorite shirt. He slapped his thigh, wondering if she could feel it. It hurt him too much to try again.

The dog was watching him from the bedroom door. It showed him its pointed tooth again. He dressed hurriedly. "All right, all right," he said, "I'm going out! Just a minute." He found the black socks in her underwear drawer, and his loafers (she hadn't polished them in more than a month. How could that be?) in the closet among a jumble of her shoes. The dog growled when he rifled her purse. "I need money to go out, don't I?" he demanded. The growl lowered, but it kept coming. Adam ignored it. Amelia had twenty-six dollars in her wallet, and a smudgy driver's license with a short-haired photo of her on it. If he got stopped, he always said he was a male impersonator. He looked enough like her to pass, which was an uncomfortable thought. She was so unattractive. But most of that was the way she carried herself, always flinching, eyes downcast; her wardrobe was full of dark, neutral colors.

He took her keys. As he walked past the growling dog, he kicked out at it, but missed. Its growl rose to a bark. It snapped at his leg, then backed off, following him at two paces until he reached the door. "Goodnight, sucker," he said as he locked the door from outside. "I hope you drank two gallons of water."

The little dark man with glasses was peeking out his door in the downstairs apartment, the way he always was. Adam made kissy lips at him. Anybody was fair game on Adam's nights—the more disgusting and repulsive the better. The little man ducked inside and slammed the door, and Adam smiled.

Amelia lay quiet, her eyes shut. His hateful clothes were tight around her hips, across her breasts, and she smelled alcohol and at least two different perfumes on Adam's shirt; the castor oil scent of lipstick came from his collar where it nudged her cheek. She could feel the sickness gathering in her stomach and knew that soon she would need to dash to the bathroom to throw up everything: the knowledge of what the monster had done the night before (she couldn't really remember, but she knew it was awful), and the remnants of whatever he had eaten and drunk.

She gulped twice.

She realized there was a strange sound in the room.

Breathing.

Terror stilled her breath, her heart. Her hands clutched the sheet.

The breathing went on, undisturbed.

So he had done it. He had finally brought his prey home. She had a horrible moment wondering what might be in her stomach besides normal food and drink. Her gorge rose. She couldn't hold back any longer. She stood up in a rush, locked herself into the bathroom, and made it all the way to the toilet before she lost it.

When she had finished retching and loosened all the most torturous buttons on Adam's clothes, she rinsed her face in the sink. Something nagged at her. There was something she was forgetting, but she couldn't think, not with some stranger in her bedroom. She got her oversize red terrycloth robe from the hook on the bathroom door and put it on over her half-undone clothes, then peeked around the door.

A man was sleeping curled in her bed, a naked man. A long lanky leg lay folded on top of the quilt, and a long arm curled around his dark head; the rest of him was drawn up around his stomach. He breathed softly, not snoring the way she expected all men to snore.

What was she going to do?

Get some decent clothes, dress quietly, grab her purse and flee the apartment. Maybe if she waited long enough the man would leave, and then she could get back in and lock up. But he knew where she lived . . .

And what about—

What about Joe?

The baby's morning wail of hunger rose just then. Amelia watched, wide-eyed, as the man in her bed yawned and stretched, then turned to look at her.

It was Kelly, Mr. Patterson from downstairs. *He knew who she was:* that was her first frozen thought.

Joe, used to being taken care of any time he made a sound, wailed a little louder.

Mr. Patterson sat up and yawned into the back of his wrist. "He's probably hungry," he said. "I couldn't find anything to feed him last night."

"What are—what are—" She hid her eyes with her sleeves.

"Well, excuuuse me," said Mr. Patterson. A minute later, he said, "You can open your eyes again. I'm covered by a sheet."

Hot tears streaked down Amelia's cheeks. She lowered the sleeves of her robe and glanced at him to see if he was lying, but he wasn't. He had a sheet up around his waist, shielding her from seeing the monster part of him. "Why aren't you wearing any clothes?" she asked, a little girl's voice coming from her mouth.

"Don't you remember anything about last night?"

Tearblind, she shook her head.

"Wait a second, that didn't come out right. Nothing happened between us last night, Amelia. Except you wanted somebody to take care of the baby on Change Night, and I guess I was the only person you could think to call."

"Change Night?" she whispered.

"Moon Night, some call it."

"Curse Night." She licked a tear off her lip and peered at him through salt haze. "How do you know about Curse Night?" He smelled like something she wanted for breakfast, and she didn't understand that at all.

"I change too."

Joe wailed a little louder. Amelia stuffed her sleeve into her mouth and bit down. What kind of monster had she left the baby with last night? She dashed through the living room and into Joe's closet. He was red-faced and teary, but when she picked him up, he settled down immediately. He didn't even smell wet. She went to the metal chair and sat, settling Joe on her thigh and offering him a breast. He sucked as if he were starving.

Mr. Patterson walked out of the bedroom, wearing the sheet like a toga. He glanced at her nursing Joe, shielded his eyes with a hand, and bent to pick up some clothes lying folded on the rug. "What bit you?" he said. He turned his back to her.

"I don't know." She heard the despair in her voice and wished she could unsay it. Her mother had taught her never to let a man hear her despair.

"How long have you been changing?"

"Since I was twelve." She hesitated. "It stopped while I was pregnant with Joe."

"How old are you now?"

"Twenty-one."

"Do you know what you change into?"

She shuddered. "A monster," she said, and then whispered, "him."

"Do you remember being him? I remember being my other self. I'm not as different, somehow, as you are."

"I can't remember anything he does. I just know it's disgusting."

"Oh," said Mr. Patterson. He didn't say anything more for a little while. "I'm going to dress in your bathroom, all right? I think the less Peter-the-snoop has to talk about, the better."

While he was gone, she got an extra diaper and draped it over Joe as he nursed so that no secret part of her showed. Her despair was so strong she worried about it getting into the milk and hurting Joe.

In a couple minutes Mr. Patterson came out. With him dressed and herself covered she could look at him again. "Mr. Patterson," she said in a low voice. Her worry about Joe made her strong enough to speak.

"Yes, Amelia."

"What do you change into?"

"A wolf. Kind of a wolf, anyway. Much more normal than your change, I imagine."

"I left the baby with a wolf?" The warmth of Joe against her chest, his hot mouth on her breast, reassured her. "How could I?"

He lifted his eyebrows, but didn't answer.

Of course, her monster self would do anything.

"How did you change his diapers?"

"It was tricky," said Kelly. He glanced at the clock above the card table where she ate all her meals. "Got to get to the site, Amelia. Gotta pick up a few things from my apartment and get to work. I'll be home after five—three hours before moonrise, more or less. We can talk then." He put his hand on the doorknob.

Joe, warm and dry, lay in her arms. "Mr. Patterson. Thanks," said Amelia. She lowered her eyes.

She locked and bolted the door behind him, not sure if she wanted to talk to him ever again. He had seen the worst part of her—if it was really part of her, and not some alien creature that took her over three nights a month, which was what she told herself, how she lived with it.

Maybe, if she worked fast, she could load everything she really needed into her VW Bug and get away, far away. There was still a little left of her mother's legacy, enough for first-and-last-plus-damage-deposit and another six months of low rent and generic groceries. After that, Joe would be old enough to go to daycare, and she could get back to temping.

But there was still the problem of getting a sitter for Joe before tonight.

Joe was sleeping against her breast. She transferred him

gently to his crib and closed the closet door almost all the way, then went to the phone.

What had happened to that girl who was supposed to come last night, anyway? Amelia had left Joe with her a few times before when she had to go shopping and couldn't take Joe. She had found the girl's number on the bulletin board at the laundromat, and the girl had been clean and prompt and had had no objections to the idea of staying with the baby overnight if necessary. The nights Patty had come when Change hadn't happened, Amelia had gone out to a movie and then come home, dismissing Patty early.

She checked the pad of paper by the phone and called the number. "Patty?" she said when a young voice answered.

"Patty's not here," said the voice, breathless. "There was an accident."

"Goodness, is she hurt?"

"Yeah, pretty bad. Yesterday she hit a car with her bike! She got a concussion. She had to go to the hospital."

"Oh, I'm so sorry! Will she be okay?"

"We think so," said the voice. It sounded uncertain.

"I'm sorry," Amelia said again. It didn't seem like the right time to ask the voice to recommend another babysitter. "I'm sorry," she said again. "Good-bye."

"Good-bye," said the voice.

She couldn't trust Joe with someone she had never met, and that included . . . Him. Adam.

She wished she knew the phone number of the place where Mr. Patterson worked. She glanced toward the closet where Joe slept, then sat on the floor, elbows on the seat of one of the chairs, chin propped on hands. She had to think.

Kelly was carrying a sack full of Chinese take-out when he knocked on Amelia's door after work. The door opened a crack and she peeked out, then widened the opening just enough for him to slip inside. He glanced at her as she bolted the door behind him, and got a shock. She had done something to her long brown hair—pinned it up somehow, the Search for Sophistication. She was wearing makeup—too much of it—and a nightgown. A flannel nightgown, but the hem was torn off above her knees, and she had rolled the sleeves up to mid-forearm, and left the buttons at the throat undone.

He had a sinking feeling.

She looked at his face, then dropped her gaze. Her pinkened lower lip trembled. "I was afraid—" she said.

He went to the table and took the white cartons out of the sack, with napkins and two pair of chopsticks. "Have you eaten yet?"

"No, Mr. Patterson."

"Come on over and sit down. Call me Kelly. You did last night."

"Last night I was desperate."

"You look pretty desperate now."

She sat down in her second chair. She wouldn't meet his eyes. "I had this great idea," she said in a small voice. "When it turned out my babysitter was in an accident. I thought . . ."

He handed her a pair of chopsticks and a carton of shrimp-fried rice. Savory steam rose from the opened carton. She set the carton down and stared at the chopsticks, still safe in their red paper sheath. "I mean, I could ask you to sit with Joe again, but you must have other things to do with your time. So I thought . . ," she said.

He opened a couple more cartons, waiting.

"I know how to get rid of Adam now," she said.

"How?"

"Get pregnant." Her glance darted up to meet his, then

dropped. After a silence, she said, "I don't know how it happened last time. How or who. But I thought . . ."

Kelly swallowed. He let a minute go by. "You know that's not a long-term solution? You don't want to spend the rest of your life pregnant, do you?" She had an attractive scent; he had noticed it every time he came into contact with her. It spoke to him even when all the rest of her was posted No Trespassing. So he knew that what she was asking him wasn't impossible, but it would probably be damned uncomfortable for both of them. "Besides, you can't just plan on getting pregnant. Sometimes it takes time and work."

Her eyes closed. She had done the lids in silver, and her lashes in black. Too much of everything, but the hand that had applied the makeup had been steady and skillful.

"Can you support two kids?"

She took a deep breath and let it out. She looked like a little girl playing Mommy. She opened her eyes and stared at him, and she looked like a wood sprite. "I don't know," she said. "There's welfare, isn't there?"

"But look," he said, leaning a little closer to her across the gently steaming food. "You can't disrupt your whole life just because you want to—you want to get rid of this little fraction of it. Three nights out of thirty, and you've got all your days free. What is it? Five percent of your month, that's all. You can live with it." It was a set speech. He had heard it from Sonya-the-sudden. That seemed so long ago. He wondered why he had been so upset about the whole thing. It worked out fairly well, as long as he focused during change on thinking that what he really needed to do in the night was guard his apartment and take care of it. He hadn't done much exploring yet, but he figured there was plenty of time for that.

"You don't know what he does," she said, her eyes tearbright.

74

"Acts like an asshole," Kelly said.

"Much worse things than that."

"How do you know?"

Her lips thinned. She looked away.

"You *do* remember."

"I do his laundry."

He reached across the table and touched her hand. "Amelia, do you remember?"

"No," she said, and her face tightened. In a whisper, she said, "Maybe." Louder, "Everything he does, he does just to torture me. He knows all the things I hate and he does them all. Things I can't even think of. Things that make me throw up. Things my mother told me would make God strike me dead on the spot."

Her mother? How'd her mother get into this? "Still, just three nights out of twenty-nine or so days."

"Would you say that if I told you I murdered people on my Curse Nights? Just three people a month?"

"Uh—no, nope, I guess you're right."

She looked toward the window. It was still light out. In the streets below children played a game that involved shouts, racing footsteps, and the slap of a ball against asphalt or wall.

"Mr.—Kelly, will you help me?"

"I still don't think this is your final answer, 'Melia."

"Maybe I can find some other answer, if I just have this . . . breathing room."

Before moonrise they sat naked side by side on her living room rug and waited, not sure how change would take them. Joe had been fed and diapered and put to bed, the birds circling above him. The lullaby played faintly from the closet behind them. "I don't know," Amelia said. She had her knees up and her hair down, concealing everything a bathing suit would have covered, though he had seen and touched most of her already. "Maybe if I just start acting more like—like him, he won't come anymore. Maybe if I liked doing what he did, he wouldn't do it anymore because he couldn't hurt me that way."

"Do you think that's possible? That you could like it?"

She slanted a look at him. "You smell good," she said. A silence. "I almost liked it," she said. "I'm not supposed to. I know I'm not supposed to. Mother said . . . But I think—"

Silver flame flared through him. It was Second Night, the night of no refusal. For an instant he tried to resist; but resistance made it hurt. He relaxed into it.

Moonlight spilled into the room through the open window. Wolf and woman stared at each other. She lifted a hand, and he nosed it. She stroked his head. "I think I can learn," she said.

Mint Condition

Everything around me blurred. My ears hurt, and my stomach felt like it had eaten itself. My palms and the soles of my feet itched and tingled.

Colors shifted in the wash of blur. A blue oblong took shape in front of me, intensified from watercolor wash to poster-paint density to a station wagon. It was big and boxy, the sort of car built to support two nine-foot-long surfboards, though there weren't any boards on the roof rack at the moment. I held keys in my hand. A green ball of fake fur the size of a fist dangled from the keys.

I swallowed three times as my body caught up to itself. Wished, the way I always did after a jump, that I had brought an ear pressure adjuster. Prohib tech for this era. I yawned instead.

Blue sky, hot sun, air thick with pollution and the scent of a nearby bakery—but air, my big itch, open air, right out there under the sky! Sounds formed a dense net around me, people walking and talking, traffic, a lot of distant different music from radios and maybe live, in the air or coming from buildings, a faint hush of waves washing the beach, the skirl of rollerskate wheels on sidewalk. I stood on the planet's surface, bare-headed under the sun. Delight swept through me.

I'd made it again.

I smiled and glanced down to find out what I was wearing. In the instant before materialization, the image sampler in my head had reached out for a compressed burst of media, sought out images of people who looked like I did, young and female, and adjusted my camo clothes and hair to fit local custom. The audio portion of my sampler program gave my brain's language center a quick overlay of local usage. Voila! Instant new me.

Of course, this only worked in eras that had a lot of media to sample. For earlier times we had to rely on stealth vids shot by explorers and banked in the vast CollectorCorps information library.

Hmmm. On this version of me, the hair was chin-length, and what I could see of it from the corners of my eyes told me it was flat, lusterless, and magenta. The clothes? Solid black. The top was long-sleeved, a tight shirt of shiny black material, tucked into black leather pants, and below that, I wore black thick-soled boots, with black laces that crisscrossed almost up to my knees. I wiggled my toes, felt lumpy socks inside the knee-high boots. I wondered if the socks were black.

"Hey. Give me those," said a grumpy voice.

Oh. Him. I had forgotten Scott, my partner on this trip, a man I'd only known half an hour. He'd told me to shut up three times already. Not everybody had the mental stamina to cope with my particular brand of badinage, but most people weren't as rude as Scott. Few guessed I was conducting a screening process. Scott had definitely flunked.

He stood on the other side of the car, dressed in the standard business suit of the middle-aged American male for a period from about 1930 to 2026, the navy version with off-white shirt. For guys who looked like Scott, this was a broad-tie-and-wide-lapel era, coupled with a flat-topped haircut, which his brown hair was almost too thin for.

None of what he wore suited him.

All right, I didn't mean it that way. I don't do puns. Not on purpose.

"Sissy! Give me those!" Scott said again. He held out his hand across the car roof.

I glared at him with narrow eyes, then glanced around.

Venice Beach, California, August, 1979. When you could still buy a copy of Marvel's *The Minus Men* #121 for cover price at a liquor store or bus station, if you had local currency or a reasonable facsimile. Marvel thought the series was dying, and put one of their brand new writer-artist teams on it, gave them free rein in terms of plot and concept, not knowing that in the future this team would create Marvel's longest-running, best-loved title, and that this issue, which introduced the characters who would later become a multi-media sensation, and which Marvel didn't print many copies of, would go through the roof.

Not only that, but the artist and author would be attending a science fiction convention in Santa Monica tomorrow. Right now nobody knew who they were except people from the future. Autographed copies of *Minus Men* #121? Practically nonexistent in 2059, at least until we got home with some.

So okay, not the most important mission I'd ever had. But not the least, either.

I sure liked the look of the people wandering around here. All different skin colors, from basement-living bleached to totally tan to black-coffee black. Lots of colors in the clothes, but then again, lots of black. Punk was almost passé, but the New Wave had stolen lots of its tropes. I saw spiked hair, neon-streaked hair, Rasta dreadlocks, and no hair.

Scott came around the car, stumbling a little in his shiny leather shoes. Another rookie mistake; we lived in slippers in the future, in padded underground complexes. Shoes took practice, and obviously he hadn't done his homework. "The keys," he said. "Give them to me!"

I shoved the keys in a pocket of my leather pants. Tight! They made a bump against my thigh. "No," I said.

"Can you even drive?" He looked at our car. I don't know how time tressing works. Nobody does. But the Collector-Corps scientists set it up so they can send a couple operatives and some camo-mass back, masked in blurs that divert the attention of nearby people away from our arrival nodes. Operatives come with high-powered media samplers, the samplers feed images into the camo-mass, and by the time the blurs fade into edges, there's the appropriate vehicle and the appropriate equipment for whenever and wherever the operatives are.

That's the idea, anyway. That's what the PR tells the world we do. Nobody talks about all the screwups—how Washu lost three of his toes when his matter-swap scythed him partially inside something already there, how Mingelle ended up in the middle of a Klan rally in the 1920s and was half-hanged before they pulled her home, or why Bista won't ever enter a room smaller than three meters on a side again.

Nobody talks about Helen or Crow or Shingawa or Plessy at all. If you don't come home, you get wiped out of all the records except people's memories, which is why I'm pretty particular about my memories. I hang onto them all.

Time tressing's not for sissies. Except me. I mean, Sissy is my name, not my nature. I love tressing, and I don't know why. Or maybe I do know, but it's not something I can explain. Anyway, I'm good at it. Nobody on any of my missions has ever gotten hurt. Humiliated, maybe, but not hurt.

I took another look at Scott. I couldn't figure out how his cover would fit in with our mission. Maybe his sampler was fritzing. AmBizMan on the beach? AmBizMan at a scifi con? Skewed. Seriously.

"Sure, I can drive," I said, "but on this mission, at this

time, the car is just a portable storage unit." I took a couple steps. I liked the feel of my clunky boots. I peered through the long narrow window into the station wagon's cargo space. Black instrument cases? Yep.

I went around to the car's back door and unlocked it, hauled out a guitar case. Way to get local money? Earn it in some unregulated way. Robbing banks worked, and so did picking pockets. Blur power and camo-mass made each of those options easy. But I liked busking the best. Then people knew what they were buying for the money we took from them. "Looks like you're elected to play the fiddle," I said.

"Play the what?"

I pointed to the other instrument case.

Scott looked skrawed.

"Go on. Get it out."

"What am I supposed to do with *that?* I mean, what is it?"

I put my case on the asphalt, got the fiddle case out of the back of the car, and closed and locked the door, then hid the keys in my pocket again. Why did they always send me on missions with dumb rookies? I mean, *every time.* I wondered if somebody wanted to cook me. I couldn't remember anybody I had made that mad, but sometimes you couldn't tell. "How much orientation did you miss, and who are you related to?" I asked.

Red stained his cheeks. "My sister's on the CC board," he said.

"And your big itch would be?"

He frowned and swallowed. His Adam's-apple bobbed. "Petroleum-powered vehicles," he whispered.

Fritterfrick! Ijits who had some obsession with past things kept creeping through CollectorCorps's job filters. Why did I always end up babysitting them?

"Pick up your instrument and follow me." I grabbed the

guitar case, strode toward the boardwalk and the beach.

Scott hovered anxiously at the car. "Wait," he called, and glanced frantically around at all the people. A few of them stopped to study him. Who had programmed his sampler? He was a total unblend. Nobody on the sidewalk looked anything like him.

Maybe his sampler had misjudged our arrival node. Samplers weren't supposed to be buggy. Then again, nothing else was supposed to be buggy either, and everything more or less was.

I sighed and walked back.

Scott put a hand on the car's roof. "How can we leave the car? Won't these people dismantle and steal it?"

Rookies. They thought everybody in every time period was some kind of crook. Obviously Scott hadn't done *any* of his homework. "You really should have paid more attention during orientation," I said. I picked up the fiddle case in my free hand and headed for the beach again.

"The car," he said, "the car, the car, the car—"

"Oh, eat it. It's camo-mass keyed to us. Nobody else can do a thing with it. Here." I handed him the smaller black case.

He looked grumpy again. "I don't know why you brought this. I don't even know what it is."

"You don't have to know. All you have to do is hold it and act like you're playing it. The sampler will fill in time-appropriate sounds."

"We're doing this why?"

"To pick up a little local tender so we can buy our target acquisitions."

He grumped all the way to the boardwalk. All right, it wasn't really a boardwalk, it was a wide concrete walkway with muscle boys, bikini girls, rollerskaters (pre-rollerblade), joggers, shoppers, coffee-drinkers, walkers, skateboarders, and leashed dogs on it. On the town side of the walk, there were all kinds of funky little shops and sidewalk cafes mingled with funky little two- or three-story apartment buildings. On the ocean side, there was a line of palm trees and light poles and green trash barrels, and beyond that, a pale beige beach churned with the footprints of thousands and supporting a batch of tan-seeking, cancer-collecting, bathing-suited bodies between us and a beautiful blue ocean. Oiled up muscleboys worked out as I watched. Younger people whooped and yelled and played Frisbee. A whole spectrum of people played in the water, facing the waves.

I stood for a moment looking at a civilization that still lived above ground. Maybe Scott had a thing for gas-powered engines—and he did, he had leaned toward every parked vehicle we had passed, sniffing as if he could snort exhaust and the scent of sun on hot metal; every time we saw a moving car, fascination glued Scott to the sidewalk, staring.

Me, I liked the sky. So strange to have air lying around free for everybody, whether you paid for your allotment or not. 'Kay, so it wasn't scrubbed or anything. But it was right out here in the open. People didn't even need breathing apparatus.

A couple of winos sat under a nearby palm tree. One was asleep, and the other looked at us. Or more like he stared at me, then took a swig from a bottle in a brown paper bag.

I crossed the boardwalk, laid down my guitar case, brushed aside a few cigarette butts, beer bottle caps, and pop-tops in the sand, and slumped between a couple of palm trees. I pressed my thumbs to the clasps holding the guitar case closed.

"Hey, man. Whatcha doing?" asked a scruffy local. He had filthy bare feet, grease-streaked jeans with holes at the knees and the bottoms of the pockets, and a denim jacket with clusters of safety pins all over it. His hair was long, blond, snarled, and dirty, and his eyes were bloodshot.

"Setting up," I said.

"Whoa. The people who live in the building across the walk, they're uptight assholes. They narc on anybody who makes noise nearby."

"Oh." I smiled at him. "Where should we go?"

"You got a permit?"

"No."

He chewed his lower lip for a minute, then said, "Follow me."

I sealed my case shut and rose as my native guide headed down the walk.

Scott, who had been standing there like an ijit—why didn't he glance around and realize that no one else in sight stood still and stared at anything with such a stupid look on their face?—grabbed my arm. "Sissy!"

I jabbed my defense fingernail into the back of his hand, and he let go fast. I had a selection of irritants and poisons I could use with the nail; I chose a minor itch. No matter how annoying Scott was, he was still my partner, and I kept my partners intact even if they were useless. "Stop grabbing me," I said. I followed the Local, and Scott ended up following me.

We came to a spot across from a coffee shop with tables on the walk in front of it. "This place is good for a little while," said Local. "If you sound good, the coffee-drinkers will give you something. You see cops coming, you make all your stuff disappear. You're not planning to be here long, are you?"

"No. Thanks!"

" 'Cause I know some other people who panhandle here. I don't want to give away their spot, man. But Gracie, she's sleeping in today."

"We won't be here long."

"Cool."

I wished I had something to give him, but we hadn't come with much of anything. I had an armband with enough nutritabs inside it to keep me eating for a month, but that was definitely prohib tech. No sharing, period.

I got my guitar all the way out of the case this time. In this time and place, the guitar was acoustic: pale, almost silvery wood with an ebony fingerboard, and a black plastic pick guard emblazoned with white dancing skeletons. The strap was now black with woven green and purple lizards crawling up it. I loved this version of me.

Local shoved his hands into his pockets and leaned up against a palm tree. "Cool guitar. What kind of stuff you play?" he asked.

"Wait and see," I said. I did know how to play my instrument; pursuing that was one of my personal quirks. On a mission, though, I usually trusted my sampler to supply me with material. Couldn't sing some song that wouldn't be popular until two years later—what if the person who was going to play it into a hit stole it from me, and I had stolen it from him to begin with? Who had ever written it? We tried never to set such question loops into action. They could stretch and snap, and then everybody would wake up in a different reality. I was kind of attached to this one.

And there was the other option, that I'd play something I knew was good and it would be totally foreign to when I was, and nobody else would like it.

I'd done a little research, enough to know that this was the era of Blondie, the Clash, the B52s, the Police, the Ramones, Talking Heads, Elvis Costello, all people I had never heard of until I pulled a fast sample out of the CollectorCorps data files and headjammed it before I left on this mission. None of what I heard seemed like something I could do with just my voice, an acoustic guitar, and the possible addition of Scott on a fiddle, so I decided to try something from an earlier era. "You like folk songs?" I asked Local.

"Folk songs?" He looked alarmed.

"They're great. All blood and death and stuff." I set the open case beside the walkway, hoping people would drop money in. "I'll play you a folk song." I slipped the guitar strap over my head, pulled a pick out of a pickholder on the guitar's side, and strummed an intro with only minimal help from the sampler. I sang the first line of "Banks of the Ohio," about a chipper so crazed with love that when his girl said no, he killed her.

"Whoa," whispered Local. He stared at my mouth while I sang, with brief glances at my breasts.

People strolling by behind him stopped, gathered. Change jingled into the open guitar case. A few people dropped paper money. Scott stood there like a mannequin, the violin case forgotten in his hand, his mouth hanging open.

I wrapped up the song with a repeat of the creepy chorus, then smiled at everyone who had stopped to listen. A few of them clapped. Most of them moved on.

Local said, "Awesome, man. Great voice."

"Thanks." I checked the guitar case. Not bad for a three-minute song. Already we could afford comic books and some of the more exotic local foods. Slurpees, maybe. I'd seen ads for those when I was in a similar time period before, but I'd never managed to taste one. I strummed an A chord. Folk songs could work—I'd try "House of the Rising Sun" next. I picked an E minor chord.

"Well," said Scott.

I glanced at him. Why was I doing all the work? What was he here for, anyway? The sampler could supply some ominous fiddle in this song. "Get out your instrument."

"Sissy. Sniggle," Scott said.

My muscles locked. My left hand gripped the guitar's neck so hard I felt the guitar strings digging into my fingernails, and the fingers on my right hand curled into claws on the strings above the sound hole.

Unwelcome knowledge flooded my system. I remembered . . . other missions. All these lame gropers I kept getting stuck with, time after time! One of them had some kind of masterword he passed on to the next, and the next, and the next. At some point in my training with CollectorCorps, somebody had wired an "obey" circuit into me. Illegal! Criminal! Horrible and humiliating!

Now I remembered every single one of those horrible missions. I had started each one feeling as though I was in charge, shepherding around some lame-o rookie on a quest to pick up this or that small perfect item for some elite who could afford the outrageous price CC would charge. Somewhere along the way, my irritating partner would whisper the magic word, and I would freeze up until he told me what he wanted.

I couldn't move. I felt the red in my face, though. There were lots of fast ways to make unregulated money besides busking, picking pockets, or bank robbing. Turning tricks, for instance.

One or two of my rookies had been—less horrible than the others. I didn't have much hope for Scott.

They always made me forget afterward.

I wished now that they wouldn't. I would be better off if I didn't sneer at them and insult them and order them around early on, wouldn't I?

But I didn't want to live with what I had gone through.

All I had to do was get through the next forty-eight hours, until the autoreturn pulled us back. If Scott followed the pattern, he, too, would tell me to forget everything. We would return to the future with what I would think was the object of our quest, and I would rest up, ignoring the bruises and small illnesses and outbreaks I always picked up on missions. Somebody would give me another assignment. I would do my homework. Then I'd lead some other lawbreaking lamebrain back into the past, and . . .

"Sissy," said Scott. "Put the guitar away."

"Hey, man. I want to hear more!" Local said.

But I had already bent to stow my guitar in its case. That was a mercy. It gave me hope, even though I dropped the guitar right on top of the money, since Scott hadn't told me to take the money out first. At least he was letting me put away my instrument instead of ordering me to abandon it. I thumbed the clasps closed.

"Let's go," said Scott.

"Hey! Male chauvinist pig. Stop bossing her around!" Local grabbed my arm.

"Drop him," Scott said.

I tapped the back of Local's hand with my defense nail, letting him have a little shot of sleep. His grip on my arm relaxed, and he fell slowly to the ground.

"Good work. Come on." Scott turned away and headed up the walk.

I followed, but glanced back at Local. I hoped he would be all right. I didn't always find such nice people on these trips.

At the car, Scott made me give him the keys, made me sit in the passenger seat while he drove. Right there I had a clear demonstration of the fact that no matter how much time you spent on a simulator, real life worked differently. Since cars were Scott's big itch, I had thought he'd be really good at them. But even in a camo-car, he couldn't drive well. He stalled and stalled again. He didn't understand 1979 traffic controls. He ran red lights and stop signs, and brought us close to death time and again.

He made me navigate with a map he had torn from a telephone book. Destination? The nearest Cadillac dealership.

Gradually I relaxed.

Maybe this wouldn't be such a bad mission.

"See that Eldorado?" Scott said, his voice alive with excitement as he pulled into the lot. "See that one? Omyglot, see that one over there? Front-wheel drive, four-wheel independent suspension, and an electronic fuel-injected V8 engine. Cadillac pioneered those features in American cars! Sweet!" He parked our camo-car across two parking spaces and jumped out, leaving the key in the car and the engine running. And me, in the passenger seat, disabled by a stupid word that didn't even mean anything except "You will now obey my every command."

A young salesman in a suit just like the one Scott wore came out of the showroom, smiling. "Hello, sir," he said, shaking hands with Scott. "I'm Bert James. How may I help you?"

"I'd like a test drive," Scott said, his voice breaking.

"Excellent. While you're enjoying a ride in one of our automobiles, though, don't you think your own fine car should be shut down?" The salesman leaned in and fished around for the key, which wasn't on the steering column the way a person from 1979 might expect. Let alone the car was keyed to Scott's and my geneprints, and wouldn't respond to anyone else. The salesman noticed me. "Hello, miss. Wouldn't you like to ride in one of our magnificent machines?"

I looked at him. On the drive over, Scott had given me permission to look around, but not to talk. In fact, he had said "shut up" a few more times, even though I hadn't said a word.

Probably to get back at me for all the talking I did right before we tressed.

"I don't recognize your car," the salesman said over his shoulder to Scott.

"It's not in general production. It's a prototype."

"Oh. Interesting! Could you please turn it off, sir? And what about your girlfriend? Maybe she'd like a test drive too?"

Scott let his breath out in a whoosh. "Oh. Yes. Probably. I guess."

The salesman straightened, and Scott leaned in and turned off the car. "Get out and come with us," he said.

I spent the rest of the afternoon in the back seat of various Cadillacs, listening to Scott and the salesman enthuse about the virtues of Cadillacs. I did find out for a fact that they had really comfortable back seats, good shocks, smooth engines, and quiet rides.

Sometimes I thought about all the carbon monoxide we were pumping into the air. Mostly, though, I thought about all the missions I'd gone on in the recent past where some ijit smoghead tongueflapping powerpusher had flipped my switch and made me dance. I thought long and hard about it. Who could have slipped me the wire? Why?

I had a half-memory of some mission before all the bad ones started. I had stepped into the tresser. The usual lights had flashed. My ears popped, the blurs washed out my surroundings, my stomach hurt, and then, floosh! Everything turned back into Now. I wondered why the mission had aborted. I'd never had one abort before—in fact, I had a reputation for luck. One of the project scientists was studying me and my luck to see if it was something they could induce in other tressers.

Able, one of the tresser programmers, had opened the

booth door. "Drink this, Sissy," he said. My stomach was still spinning and glogging. I glanced at the telltales in the tresser room and noticed there was something weird about the permachrono. Before I could figure it out, though, I drank what Able gave me. Then everything blurred.

Later I woke up in my own cubicle. My boss said I'd gotten sick before I could even go on a mission and that they'd sedated me while the sickness ran its course. That was why I lost two days.

I couldn't even remember what I was supposed to find and fetch on the aborted mission.

It had to be Able who had done this to me. Scuzzed the mission, made me lose two days while I was undergoing illegal bioengineering that turned me into a slavebot.

"Sissy," said Scott.

Able. But why? Did he hate me?

"Get out of the car, Sissy," Scott said.

After that non-mission, time after time, me and ijits, sweeping through different periods in the past so they could pet dinosaurs or gamble on a Mississippi riverboat or digi-photo gladiator games at the Coliseum. Time after time I performed for them and they told me to forget all about it, and then I got them home in perfect condition, even though I myself got a little skewed and couldn't remember how. Time after time I didn't understand the nasty smiles my partners gave me before they walked out of my life, good riddance.

How lucky was I, really?

I got out of the car.

"Straighten up and look pretty, Sissy," Scott said.

Well, that was easier said than done. Not a very tangible order, and what exactly did he have in mind? I stood tall, hunched my shoulders, relaxed them, ran my fingers through my short limp pink hair. Bert the salesman watched me.

91

Damn. I should have listened to their conversation while I was riding around in the back seat, but I had been too busy going down nightmare memory alley. What was happening now?

"Would you like to get to know Sissy better, Bert?" Scott asked the salesman. "She'll do whatever you want. Anything you ask. Won't you, Sissy? You'll do anything Bert wants."

I nodded.

Rage ran through my body like blood, and I couldn't respond to it. I couldn't walk away. I couldn't ziss damned Scott with my defense nail, and I couldn't scream my anger. Scott hadn't given me permission.

Bert took a couple steps toward me.

"I'll just take this Eldorado out for a little spin. Back in half an hour," Scott said. He jingled the keys in his hand, then climbed into the big car we had just been riding around in.

Bert came slowly to me. He stared at my lips. Then down at my breasts. His tongue darted out to lick his upper lip.

Scott started the car, put it into reverse, and almost ran over us. Bert shoved me out of the way, grabbed me before I crashed. "Hey!" Bert yelled after Scott.

Scott burned rubber on his way out of the parking lot.

One of the other salesmen came out of the showroom then, looked after Scott's taillights, glanced at Bert. "It's all under control," Bert said. His voice shook. "Come on, Sissy. I'll get you some coffee."

I followed him through the showroom into a warren of offices. He actually got me a cup of coffee from a big pot, and added cream and sugar. "You okay?"

I would do anything Bert wanted; Scott had instructed my wired self to follow Bert's orders. Obviously, Bert wanted me to answer his question. Maybe he even wanted to have a conversation with me.

Yeah. That could work.

I gulped some coffee. It was really good coffee, made with real beans, unlike anything we could mimic in the future. "Sorta," I said at last.

"Come on back to my office. We can discuss sales details."

Bert led me past a couple of receptionist stations and the dealership's auto repair shop to a small windowless office with a desk and two chairs, one behind the desk and one in front of it. The office was twice the size of my home cubicle, and the furniture was permanent instead of zipout. I knew he wouldn't have comforts like self-adjusting lights, self-styling color schemes for the fabrics—well, actually, he didn't even have fabrics—or self-adjusting hardness on the surfaces. Still, I liked the office.

The room smelled deliciously of cigarette smoke.

Bert locked the door and went around to the big chair behind the desk. I sat in the other chair and finished my coffee, sipping slow to delay whatever came next. Bert watched me. Finally I put my Styrofoam cup down on his desk.

"Will you really—" Bert coughed and stared at the surface of his desk, which had a scatter of paperwork across it.

I sighed. Scott's instructions hadn't been particularly lucid. "What do you want, Bert?"

His gaze flashed up. His eyes looked hungry. "You are one top-of-the-line babe," he said. "I've never made it with a punk chick before."

I felt weird shifting and swirling inside. Scott had told me to do whatever Bert wanted. Bert wasn't very clear on what he wanted, but if I could jump the gun and give him what he was *going* to want before he even got around to saying it, maybe I could introduce a little free will into the equation.

I rose. I perched on the edge of his desk, then swung my

legs up and slithered across the desk toward him, scattering papers. He sat back in his chair, his eyes growing wider. I ran my tongue across my lips.

"Okay," Bert said. "But—"

I leaned forward, and he backed up. The chair was on wheels. It slammed into the wall behind him.

"I don't—" Bert's face glowed bright red.

Hey. Maybe he didn't want me after all. I pulled back, sat cross-legged on his desk, and studied him.

"I mean," Bert said. He inched the chair forward again with his toes. "You're beautiful. Sleek and stylish. Great features. But I, uh,—" Then he whispered, "This is just like those letters to *Penthouse*. What's wrong with me?"

"You're nice," I said.

Bert turned even brighter red. He coughed. "Well, uh, you don't, uh."

I waited. I wondered if I could have some more coffee. I was liking this situation a lot. It was so much more benign than a lot of the unwelcome memories that had crowded into my brain when Scott said "sniggle" to me.

Bert struggled. "You're not going to tell, uh, Scott, uh—"

"I'll tell him whatever you want me to."

"You'll tell him I was a giant stud?"

"If that's what you want."

Bert turned to stare at a calendar on the wall. It showed a scenic view of the Grand Canyon. I had seen lots of pictures of that. The real thing was just another underwater feature in my time.

"Say, Sissy?" Bert said after a little while.

"Yes?"

"Is Scott ever bringing my car back?"

I blinked. "I don't know. I never worked with him before."

"Oh, God." Bert got to his feet. "I should never have

94

handed him those keys. I never even looked at his driver's license. I wonder if I should call the cops."

I checked my wristwatch. "He said he'd be back in half an hour." We had forty-eight hours to complete our mission before the autoreturn kicked in; we could also end early, so long as we did enough planning. Either way, Scott and I needed to get us and our car back to that parking place in Venice. Autoreturn would work if you weren't in exactly the right place, but you couldn't count on it working well.

Bert unlocked the door and opened it. "I wonder if he will," he said.

I wondered too. I'd had partners decide to decay on me before, I now knew, with my new access to all the forbidden memories. Guys who had scratched their itches and only made them stronger, guys who wanted to stay in the past. They had been confident that they could make me leave them there, knowing how I was wired. And yet, somehow, I'd never lost a partner. The more I thought about it, the more I realized how rare a record like that was. Everybody I knew at CollectorCorps had lost something except me.

Bert got me some more coffee and then we went out into the lot and watched cars speeding by on the four-lane roadway with the big stoplights next to the dealership. After we'd stood outside watching traffic for a while, one of the other salesmen approached us. He looked just as suited and restrained as Bert did. "So, how do you like our new line?" Bert asked me as the other man came over.

"Awesome," I said.

"We make the best cars in the world."

"I totally believe you."

"Miss, are you interested in purchasing a Cadillac?" asked the second salesman.

"I'd like a whole fleet."

The salesman stared at me as though I was insane, then looked toward the L.A. skyline and shrugged.

I tried to look important and famous, as though I could afford a whole fleet of Cadillacs. Camo can do that for you.

"I'll cut you in on the commission, Hector," Bert said. "I'm going to talk options with Sissy now."

Hector smiled and headed back to the showroom.

The green Cadillac Eldorado pulled into the parking lot and stalled, which you'd think no one could make a Cadillac do. It shuddered, shook, and stopped. Scott got out.

"Bert," I said.

"Sissy."

"Do me a favor?" Scott was coming toward us. He smiled and smiled.

"For a favor," Bert said.

"Tell me: 'Whatever happens, Sissy, don't forget, this time.' "

"Huh?"

"Please. Just say it."

"Okay. Whatever happens, Sissy, don't forget, this time."

Something fast as fire and sour-sweet shocked its way through me. Take that, wire!

"Sissy?" Bert said.

"Thanks." I put all my heart into it.

"Will you tongue-kiss me?"

"Sure."

In full view of Scott and everybody in the showroom, I gave Bert the tongue-kiss of a lifetime. We both tasted of coffee and desperation. In that moment I loved Bert more than anyone I'd ever known.

"Sniggle!" said Scott from behind us.

I brushed Bert's tongue with mine one last time before I let him go.

"Give it up, Sissy. You're back on my time. Let's go. We have work to do!" Scott sounded mad.

Meanwhile, Bert was excited. "Will you marry me?"

"No, honey. But thanks for asking." Wait. How could I say no to Bert when Scott had told me to do whatever Bert wanted? I guessed the new orders canceled the old ones.

Bert gave me a really sweet smile and turned to Scott. "So, Mr. Madrone, have you decided on a color for your Cadillac?"

"Why don't you give me a brochure that outlines all my options, and I'll get back to you?"

Bert went inside and got a full-color brochure. "This explains all our options and has color chips," he said.

"Thanks, Bert." Scott took the brochure, grabbed my arm, and dragged me back to our car, where he handed me the keys. "I'll call you tomorrow," Scott yelled over his shoulder. I took one more look at Bert. Bert blushed and waved his fingers. I waved mine.

"Get in and drive," Scott said.

Night had drifted in while Scott was off battling traffic and I was teasing Bert. I climbed into our car's driver's seat. I glanced at Scott, wondering why he was letting me drive.

"After a while, it was too much," Scott said. "They're crazy out there."

I started the car, flicked on the headlights, and pulled out onto the road. I wondered where Scott wanted to go, but I didn't want to ask him, in case he told me to shut up again. I liked being able to converse.

Scott slumped in his seat.

Since he didn't give me any directions, I drove us back to Venice and parked in the very spot where we had arrived that morning. Then I sat there staring at people through the windshield. In the night, the music from bars with open doors was louder, and there were more tourists and locals wandering the street.

Scott sat silent for a long time. Then he said, "I now return control of this mission to you, except stop bossing me around all the time, and forget everything that's happened today. When I say the word, you'll think we've just arrived. No, that won't work. You already got the money. You'll remember the part about singing on the sidewalk, only you'll think it happened at night, and that we can go into the next phase right now. Forget everything that happened since I said sniggle this morning. Ready? Three . . . two . . . one . . . sniggle."

I felt extremely odd. Little clicks pinged my brain. I clung to Bert's command. No matter what happened, I wouldn't forget this time. And I didn't forget; but the knowledge kind of dropped away. I sat up and said, "What are we doing in the car? We have a comic book to buy." I went to the back of the car, opened it, opened my guitar case, and fished money out from under my guitar. "Come on."

Scott got out and followed me. We went to a head shop and found five copies of *Minus Men* #121, all in mint condition. I bought them and slipped them into protect sleeves I had brought with me, along with the receipt for authentication, and then Scott and I went to supper.

How strange, I thought, how strange, as I sleepwalked through the rest of the mission, on the surface my usual self, and underneath turning over all my new and horrible knowledge. We slept in the car and washed up at a public restroom on the beach the next morning. I got us into the convention hotel where the scifi con was being held. I managed to sneak us into the bar when the author and artist went there; we didn't have to pay a membership fee to the convention or go to any of the programming; I had memorized target faces before we tressed, the way I always did. The boys were flattered to be asked for autographs.

"Listen," I said. "This is going to be really big. You guys are going places."

They looked at each other and laughed, and bought me and Scott drinks. It was their first big convention, and nobody else had recognized them. Travis, the artist, had actually told a dealer who stocked *Minus Men* in the dealers' room that he was the artist on issue #121, and the dealer had asked him to sign all the copies in stock. Later Travis dragged Milton the writer back with him, and Milton had signed the comics too. "But it doesn't feel real when you make it happen yourself," Travis said.

"Don't worry. I bet this is the last convention where nobody knows who you are."

They laughed. Milton knocked on the wooden bar for luck. I said good-bye for me and for Scott, who was mostly silent and grumpy. We went back to our car, and I hit the autoreturn button, and we went home.

After debriefing, the boss congratulated me on another mission well run and took away my comic books. I went to the public bath and soaped and soaked, soaped and soaked, three times, trying to scrub off all the memories. Yet I didn't really want to lose them. I felt amazed and pleased that I had managed to get around the wire and keep what was mine, no matter how awful.

Now what?

Stick my defense nail through Able's throat? Complain to one of the senior staff, start a criminal investigation? What if the senior staff were in on this? Should I just shut up and keep working the way I always had?

Or get out of the business, join my sib's hydro food farm? My sib and I had always been close, and she had never approved of my career. She would be pleased if I gave it up. I knew she'd accept me in her enclave if I asked. Plus, I had assets. I had banked lots of air and water. CollectorCorps paid me very well for my perfect record.

I went home. I set my cubicle walls to old growth forest, complete with bird, wind, and insect sounds, and sat for a long time on my sleep shelf, watching sun slant down through redwood branches to touch mossy ground. I gave myself a couple hits of enriched air.

If I never tressed again, I would never again stand on the planet's surface and look up at the sky without a faceplate. Never again taste all the biodiversity there used to be, never drink coffee made from real beans again, never talk again to people who hadn't grown up in holes in the ground.

How could I keep tressing? There was camo-me, the one who pretended she didn't remember anything, and mint condition me, but she was only a cover over the blemished me who now knew what was inside. Sure, I forgot every time; but I remembered every time in between forgetting. Two Sissies were living their lives in alternating stripes, and one of them got sicker and sicker of everything.

Around three a.m. I switched my walls over to Venice Beach, California, 1979. Sun, sand, people. These were views my sampler had taped while I was there; I always debriefed my sampler into the CC information library as soon as I got home, but I'd never accessed my own records before. Deja deja very vu.

I searched for Scott's sampler recordings. There were walls to prevent my accessing something I wasn't coded for, but I hacked through them. Now I knew why he had showed up in a business suit; he'd preprogrammed his sampler to find an image of him that a car dealer would pay attention to. Now I knew why he was so grumpy. His driving was terrible. He had been ticketed and almost arrested by police three times in the course of his solo test drive. His taste of real cars hadn't matched his dream of driving at all.

I jumped to my own backlog and fastscanned back to the aborted mission I barely remembered.

My sampler had watched everything as Able set me up, even the events that happened while I was sedated. Able and another programmer had worked me over together.

It was in my record. Along with every missing segment of my memory. I headjammed them all, confirmed what I had learned on my last mission. Some of it was horrible. Some people I had worked with did not deserve to be called people.

It was all in my record. Senior staff had to know. The guy studying my luck probably knew. How many people knew?

I ran off a copy of my whole record with CC, put it on a passive physical medium, sewed it into the lining of my jacket.

In the morning I went to my boss and said I needed some time off.

"Any special reason?" she asked.

"I need a break."

She asked me again. I said I had vacation time coming to me. She shook her head, but she let me go.

I took a tube out to my sib's place.

After two weeks there, I was ready to shoot everyone I knew. I did drop my nephews twice with my nail's mildest sleep, even though my sib got really mad the first time. They were not restful children, though.

My worst problem was skysickness. I hadn't gone so long without seeing sky in years.

So of course in the end I went back to work. Somehow my partner on my next mission ended up with his hand badly cobra bitten, though. I let go of my luck and kept hold of my memories.

On every mission, no matter what else happens, I open my arms to ancient skies.

Night Life

Nothing above ground tastes so good as fairy food, and no human man is as beautiful as those who dwell below. No daytime music sounds so sweet as the music of the fairy ball.

Every night I and my eleven sisters snuck down the secret tunnel beneath my oldest sister's bed. We passed through the grove of silver-leafed trees, and the grove of golden-leafed trees, and the grove of diamond-leafed trees, and then we came to the dance hall, all light and color and music unimaginably beautiful, where our cavaliers waited for us.

I, Marzia, am the youngest, and first went to the dance when I was twelve. I began sleeping in the big room with my sisters when I was eight, and every night my sisters gave me a sleeping posset until they judged me old enough to join them.

For those four years, I, like everyone else in the castle, only knew my sisters did something every night that wore out their slippers. The mystery of it maddened our father.

My first time underground, four different fairy men led me out to dance, each teaching me more than any of my father's dancing masters ever had. Like my sisters, I wore through the leather soles of my dancing slippers and had to commission a new pair the next morning.

After I had been going belowground four years, I found the one of all of them I wished to dance with. His name was Fern, and I found him among the musicians, which is odd when you think about it; every dancing man I met there was wonderful to talk to, beautiful to look at, excellent to dance with. Yet my eye was drawn to Fern, though he never danced, but always played his lap harp.

Some of the musicians were aboveground folk the fairies had heard and desired because of their skill with instruments, and enticed or kidnapped into the kingdom. Some few were fairies themselves. It seemed the fairy folk lived for pleasure and delight; music-making was too much like work for most of them. I heard it whispered that Fern was half mortal, but that did not dim his beauty a whit.

I watched Fern, and saw that he watched me, even though he never came out from behind his instrument those four years. Finally in a lady's choice dance, I chose him, and he could not refuse me, though his fingers clung to his instrument.

His feet did not know the dance. I took him away from the main chamber to one of the side halls, the one with the crystal stream and the ice statues. We could still hear the music, but few others saw us. There I taught Fern the steps to riddle the rose and the leader follows.

At first Fern was angry with me for pulling him away from making music, but later, when we had several nights' practice behind us and could dance together, he said, "This is good. This is another way of knowing the music." He pressed a kiss to my forehead.

I thought then that I knew my future. Foolish as I was, I did not watch my sisters, who changed partners a dozen times a night.

Foolish I was not to remember that however dull daytime life was, it still had the power to invade the nights.

We were all twelve nodding over our embroidery frames the next afternoon when my sister Aprilla poked me with her needle hard enough to draw blood.

I jerked awake and looked at her, my needle raised, ready

to cross needles with her, but she said, "Hist! I have it from the cobbler's boy that Father has been searching for a spy again, inviting anyone to come and catch us in our journey. He promises marriage to one of us and half the kingdom to the man who discovers where we go at night."

I tapped Maya on my other side, and whispered the news to her, and she tapped Junia, until we all knew the same thing. Yarnmistress Teazel was sleeping and noticed nothing.

My father had recruited spies before, but we had always defeated them. Usually it was as simple as having whichever of us caught the spy's eye offer him a sleeping posset before we went to bed.

Once or twice a spy resisted, and then Septima practiced an art she had learned from one of her cavaliers, casting confusion or fairy sleep over the spy, and then we went belowground as usual.

At supper that night we were not surprised to see that a strange man sat at our father's right hand. He wore dirt-colored cotton clothes instead of velvet and silk, and his skin was dark with sun. He kept his head down over his food, nodded when Father addressed him, and hesitated over his answers. Unused to speaking with royalty, I thought.

He glanced at me and I saw silver in his eyes.

Fern had just such silvery glints in his eyes.

I trembled and clasped Maya's hand under the table. I feared that this spy would not be easy to evade.

After supper and entertainment, my sisters and I, as usual, retreated to our room upstairs.

"His eyes were for you," Febria told me as we brewed the posset. "So you shall give this to him."

"He will not be tricked," I said. "He is different from the others."

Septima gathered the powdered pearl, fern seed, and

pieces of nutshell she would need for her art. "If he will not be tricked, he will be bespelled," she said. "Don't worry."

Presently the stranger came up to the little room beside ours, the one where our father always stationed his spies. It had a door that led to our room, and the lock was on the stranger's side.

I took the posset in a white porcelain cup. Febria sprinkled nutmeg on top. It smelled so lovely I wanted to drink it myself, and remembered the days when I had such a drink every night.

I knocked on the door, and the stranger opened it to me. Ill-mannered, he stared and stared at me as he had not at supper earlier. "S-something to ease your night," I whispered, holding out the cup to him. What if he found our secret? What if he chose one of us in marriage? Would he choose me? Febria, who knew how to watch for such signs, thought he would.

So I studied this stranger too, in smaller glances. Hard-handed, coarse-haired, narrow-mouthed, I found him. But silver in the eyes, and a smile, when he gave it, that made him beautiful.

"Thank you," he said, taking the cup from me. Finally he stopped staring. He lifted the cup to his lips.

Something clattered to the floor. I glanced toward it. A small knife, sheathed in leather, with an ebony handle. Why had it fallen, and where had it come from?

I looked back at the stranger. "Aah," he said. "Thank you. That was delicious." He held the empty cup out to me and stooped to pick up his knife.

"Sleep well," I whispered. I backed into our bedroom and handed the cup to my waiting sister, listened as the stranger closed and locked the door.

"Did he drink it?" Febria murmured.

"I don't know. It is gone, anyway."

We waited an hour and a half in silence. At the end of that time, Septima worked a charm on the lock and opened the door to the stranger's room. We saw him lying there asleep, snoring. Septima sealed the door again.

"Let's not go tonight," I whispered to the others.

"He sleeps," said Febria. "Where's the harm?"

"He makes fools of us."

But my sisters laughed at my apprehensions, and we all tugged Febria's bed aside. She sketched the sign on the floor that opened our door to the belowground world. I could hear the far-off music already, flute, harp, fiddle, and drum, and smell the fruits that hung always ripe from the trees in the metal- and jewel-leafed orchards, sweeter and juicier than any earthly fruit. The light that shone from the tunnel was the color of sun through spring leaves.

We ran down the steps, laughing. My heart yearned for Fern.

And yet, as I reached the bottom stair, something held up the hem of my skirt, as though it were caught in a crack. I tugged it loose but could see no trap.

As we crossed the silver-leafed orchard, I heard a tiny crackle behind me, as of a twig breaking.

As we traveled the gold-leafed grove, I heard such a sound again.

As we passed through the diamond-leafed grove, I heard it again.

I looked behind each time, and saw nothing but a waving branch. Since we had all plucked fruit as we passed, there was nothing significant about that.

Then we reached the dance hall and were swept into the heart of the dance. My feet were joyful to know such figures, and my eyes loved looking at the beautiful and graceful people all around me. I forgot my fears.

Not until I had been at the dance an hour did I approach Fern and coax him away from the musicians' dais. He came more easily that night. We went to the hall of flowers and I taught him face the future, and laugh lies bleeding, and over and under.

The music stopped and he held me closer and whispered in my ear, "Who is that shadow that follows you?"

All my joy fled. "It is my father's spy. He will tell my father where we go every night, and then he can claim me in marriage, and they will close our door to this world." I saw all the bright fire of music, color, dance, laughter, our cavaliers and their ladies, all I knew of wonder, fall to ash in my mind.

"No," Fern murmured, and kissed me on the lips for the first time. He tasted of sweet grass and sage. "Now I will teach you a dance," he said in a louder voice, "catch the rabbit's toe," and he put his arms around me. We whirled together, arms about each other's waists, and then he loosed me and lunged. A moment later he gripped a black cap in his hands, and my father's spy stood unveiled before us.

"Who are you?" Fern asked him.

"Prewitt, a huntsman, my lord," said the spy in a shaking voice.

Fern studied the cap he had taken from the spy. "A cap of invisibility, such as only Mist makes. Where did you get it?"

The spy had leaves from the orchard trees sticking out of the wallet on the belt at his waist. He looked confused and frightened. "An old woman in the marketplace gave it to me," he said. "She vowed 't'would help me catch the princesses and earn my fortune."

"What did she ask in return?"

"She asked nothing, but gave it to me in thanks for three coppers I gave her. She was begging."

"So it is rightfully bought," Fern said. He sighed. "Someone did this mischief a-purpose, then. Is it my Marzia whose hand you would ask in marriage?"

A small thrill went through me then. My heart had already claimed Fern, but this was the first I knew that he claimed me in return.

Prewitt said, "I find her most comely, my lord, but all of the princesses are beautiful; I would be happy with any. Though I know them not."

Fern thought for a moment, silver flashing in his eyes. At last he turned to my father's spy and said, "Let us contrive."

The following morning our father summoned us before him and confronted us with his spy.

"My daughters, where do you go each night?" our father asked us, and we all answered, "Nowhere, father, but to our room and our rest."

"That is not true, is it, my spy?" our father asked.

"It is not true. I have seen where they go," said the spy. "They go to the underground kingdom."

All my sisters gasped at this.

"They pass through a grove of silver-leafed trees." He took leaves of silver from his wallet. "They pass through a grove of gold-leafed trees." He brought out leaves of gold. "They pass through a grove of diamond-leafed trees." He added leaves of diamond to the bouquet he held. "And then they come to the fairy ballroom, and there they dance their slippers through each night."

All my sisters paled as he spoke. Only Maya looked at me and noticed I was not surprised.

"At last a man who can do as I ask," the king said. "Thank you for unearthing this mystery. Now at last we can put a stop to this wild behavior and teach these girls to be fit wives for mortal men. Choose any of my daughters as your wife, and I will grant you half my kingdom."

"Marzia is the one I want," said the spy.

I went to him and we were wed then and there. It was Fern's walnut-stained hand I held, Fern who wore Prewitt's coarse clothes in front of my father, Fern who gave me my second kiss, my first as a married woman.

Fern it was who told my father's workmen how to close the tunnel under Febria's bed that led to the underground, and Fern it was before we left the castle who opened another tunnel under Maya's bed and gave all my sisters fairy shoes that would never wear through no matter how hard they danced.

Prewitt stayed belowground and learned to dance from the fairy women. Each night he danced with a different one of my sisters, and each day he ran with the fairy huntsmen after beasts beyond legend. After a while he married my sister Maya, and by that time he had learned all he needed to know of courtliness; they spent half their time aboveground and half below.

Fern built me a castle on a hill in our half of the kingdom, and opened a door to underground there too. I saw my sisters every night, except on nights we entertained. Fern invited wandering bards and harpers to our great hall and played with the best of them. Some of them went willingly underground. Others taught him new music to take there. I learned to play the lute, and taught Fern tickle the baby and patch the roof, and we were very happy.

Entertaining Possibilities

For starters, they didn't want iced tea.

Jason set the tray holding four tall pebbled amber glasses on the coffee table. The ice swimming in the tea clinked softly against the glass sides. The long skinny spoons lying on the tray *rissed* against each other. He sighed and looked at his four unknown relatives seated around the table.

"Don't you have anything else?" asked his mother-in-law, Hazel, a stocky woman with a froth of strawberry-blonde curls around her head. She was wearing a dress that was black except for certain half-visible cabalistic symbols woven into the material that occasionally winked gray.

"What did you have in mind?" Jason said. Though he had been married to Janie for six years and they had had two children together, he had never met most of his in-laws or heard anything about them. Janie had told him exactly one thing about anyone in her family: the only time he went to see Janie in the rambling, decrepit old mansion she had called home before she and Jason ran away together, soft-skinned, wrinkled old Aunt Sophie had approached Jason on the staircase, looking harmless and pleasant, holding out her hands as if in greeting, and Janie had said, "Don't let her touch you, Jason. She has digestive enzymes in her fingertips."

Not exactly a whole character profile.

Aunt Sophie was sitting in the best armchair, her glasses glinting, her thin white flyaway hair catching evening light. She rubbed her fingertips back and forth across the chair arms, shaving the velvet down to nubs, and humming.

"Do you have any wine?" Hazel asked. "A nice *fume blanc?*"

"I'd like a good stout ale," said Zeke, who claimed to be Janie's father, though he looked way too young for that, and resembled Janie not at all. Hazel, sitting beside him on the couch, looked old enough to be his grandmother.

Sophie just hummed.

Janie's older brother Rod said, "Blood would be nice. Steaming hot if possible." He sat folded like an uncomfortable stork in the second-best armchair across from Aunt Sophie.

"I'll see what I can do," said Jason. He wished like hell that Janie were home, but she had just left with the children to walk to the corner market for milk when these people showed up on the doorstep. Perhaps they had waited for that.

What would Darrin Stephens do in a case like this? Trust to dumb luck and his own ill-placed confidence in himself, and have faith in human nature, maybe. And then he'd get in trouble.

Jason knew too much about the nature of these humans to trust them, without Janie having told him anything at all. He had lived with her for six years, through tough times and good times, and he had watched how close she came time after time to doing something really devastating to him. Getting her to stop and think had been his hardest task in their relationship. She was doing pretty well these days.

He picked up the tray and walked back into the kitchen. Wine. Ale. Blood, steaming hot. What did the tall scary thin guy who looked so much like Janie expect Jason to do, go out and kill something?

Jason got a mug, a wineglass, and a soup mug down from the cupboard and stared at them for a while. Suppose he gave these people what they wanted. That would probably just frustrate them; they wanted him to fail. So should he give them the wrong things and see what happened next?

He was pretty sure they wouldn't reward him for that, either.

He poured some Gallo white wine into the glass, opened a can of Bud and poured some of it into the mug, spooned some of yesterday's leftover tomato soup into the soup mug and put it in the microwave on high for a minute, thinking. Should he offer them cookies? They'd want caviar.

He wrapped his hands around the warm soup mug after he took it out of the microwave, smelling the fragrant steam rising from the soup. There was the faintest possibility that this mug held chicken blood; the chef at the big mansion up the hill killed her own chickens, and she might have given Jason some of the blood for his roses, and he just might have put the blood in the fridge, then gotten out a jug and poured some in this mug before he heated it.

He watched and studied the possibility until it became solid enough for him to grasp, and then he grabbed it. The steam rising from the mug shifted scents. Feeling a little sick to his stomach, Jason set the soup mug on the tray and picked up the other mug, thinking about what a mistake Budweiser had made, filling a can with fine Bavarian ale instead of just regular beer; it was a faint and faded possibility, but he went after it and caught hold. After welcoming that possibility into reality, he thought about how the wine he had poured was different, until it was.

He blew a breath up across his face, riffling his bangs, then took the tray back through the swinging door into the living room. Rod's nose wrinkled in distaste when Jason handed him the mug of blood. Hazel and Zeke sipped their beverages and stared at Jason with narrowed eyes. As he had suspected, none of them seemed pleased. Sophie was still absent with open lids.

"What made you decide to visit us?" Jason asked, sitting cross-legged on the rug and facing them all over the coffee table.

"It's time," said Hazel.

"Interesting," Jason said.

"It's time to summon Janie back home," Hazel said.

"What?" Jason blinked.

"She's had her little fling. We were certain she would give up and come home a long time ago, but she hasn't. This has gone on too long. It's time for her to come back where she belongs."

"No," Jason said.

"Ridiculous of her to even think about dating outside her species," Rod said. "Ludicrous! She's lost her mind."

"She's staying with me as long as she wants to," Jason said, and touched the tiger-striped ring he wore around his little finger. Maybe he could protect himself from these scary people, but just maybe he couldn't. Might as well summon a guardian angel or two.

A large blue-and-black swallow-tailed butterfly drifted in through the open window. It landed on the poinsettia plant next to the chair where Aunt Sophie sat. Jason nodded to it.

"She's been playing with you, boy," said Zeke. "Seems like she might even have been nice to you. But she was never here to stay." He smiled at Jason, the rueful smile of one fool to another.

"She's my wife, the mother of my children. And if you knew her at all, you'd know that she goes where she wants to go, and stays where she wants to stay. I don't think she wants to go anywhere with you people."

"You wouldn't presume to speak for her, would you?"

Hazel asked, a razor edge to her voice. "Why don't you let her decide?"

"Sure," Jason said, shrugging. "It's the only way."

"Her decision will be much easier if you aren't around when she returns," Rod said.

"Or if you're less recognizable," said Hazel.

Zeke said, "I would advise running, young man."

"This is my house," Jason said.

"Oh, no. This is Janie's house—what a pitiful little house it is, too. Not even any debris or cobwebs, and the windows open so wide and bright, and all the rooms so tiny," said Hazel. "Puny digs! Imagine our Janie settling for something so negligible! I wonder whatever got into her."

"Run away," Zeke said.

"And just let Janie come home to you people? No, I think not."

Zeke sighed.

"I wonder what sort of thing you tend toward being?" Hazel said. "People do have tendencies. I used to turn boys into fish. After doing that a while I let them decide which fish to be. One of them turned into a fugu. I thought that was clever of him. What do you suppose you tend toward?"

"That's easy," Jason said. "A plant."

"A *plant?*" repeated Rod. "How lame!"

"Maybe you're more interesting than I thought," said Hazel.

"Could be." Jason scratched his forearm.

"What sort of plant?" asked Hazel. "A daisy? A sunflower? A cabbage?"

"No. Nothing benign. Nightshade, perhaps." Jason smiled at Hazel.

She smiled back. "Lovely, but not one of your usual potted plants. I think perhaps better a miniature rose bush." She lifted her hands and wiggled her fingers at him, speaking words aloud. Her voice changed, and her words were like knives, whittling at him.

He searched for a possibility that her spell would miss him, but he couldn't find one in time. The giant butterfly flew up and hovered in the air above him, but it was startled by the woman's quickness, too. Jason curled up, trying to protect his core of self as Hazel's words cut him to pieces.

When she stopped speaking he knew he was still himself, though he wasn't centrally located any longer. His awareness ran through a lot more pieces and skinny parts than it had in a while. He felt as though he had been peeled in a narrow spiral and spread out all over the house and furniture. Nerve and muscle ran through all of him but some of it was so far away that it took longer for him to figure out what those parts were doing and feeling.

He was wrapped around a lot of things. Some of them were squirming and struggling. He thought about that and decided they must be his relatives. He clung tighter to them.

Part of him knew which direction was down and which was up, which could feed him with sunlight and which could give him water. He pushed a thousand toes down through and between barriers until he hit wet; he spread his new many fingers out until they found light to feed on. He strengthened himself and tuned in to the day's rhythm and waited.

Presently something touched him from the direction of sun. Then two other things. Their touches had a fragrance he remembered and savored, though he had never exactly sensed it this way before.

One of them bit him.

He gathered all the strength he had collected, sought out the right possibility, and drew himself back into a smaller shape, trying to remember what being human felt like.

"What's the big idea?" Janie screamed at him from the

front doorway after he had diminished himself. "We don't play those kinds of games here!"

"It wasn't—I didn't—" He gestured toward the couch and the armchairs, then glanced that way.

They were scratched and bleeding. Their clothing was in shreds. They stared at him, unblinking.

Janie pushed the children behind her and said, "What are you doing here?"

None of them answered.

Janie cocked her head. "What did you do to them?" she asked her husband.

"I don't know," said Jason. "Your mom turned me into a plant. I don't know what kind."

"It was stickery, with black thorny stems like barbed wire, and dark skinny leaves. It still tasted like you, though. And I think it was—it had buds. You're not going to flower again, are you?" She sounded irritated.

"I don't know."

"Don't. Don't even think about it." She glanced narrow-eyed at the children behind her, then gave him a glare.

"I'll try not to."

After watching him a second, she turned and knelt, then spoke gently to the boy and girl. "Stay on the porch, all right? Or you can go to the swing set, but no further unless you take a *kyre* with you, all right?"

"Yes, Mommy." Topaz, the older, took Andrew's hand in hers and led him across the lawn toward the swing set.

Janie walked into the house and went to stand beside Jason. She gripped his hand and studied her family. "What are you people doing here?"

Zeke finally shuddered and rubbed his eyes. "We came to take you home," he croaked.

"Why?"

"Because you didn't come home on your own."

"So what? I'm not going near that place. Probably forever."

"You've got to come home," Zeke said in a toneless voice.

"No I don't. Ma? Say something, Ma."

Hazel started shaking. "What happened?" she whispered after a little while.

"You turned Jason into a plant, didn't you? Why on Earth would you do a thing like that?"

"A nice potted rose. A little one," said Hazel, shivering. She looked at Jason and stilled. Her eyes were wide and full of nightmares.

"You can't turn Jason into anything small," said Janie.

"Why not?" Rod asked, his voice hoarse.

Janie glanced sideways at her husband. She pursed her lips. After a minute, she shrugged. "He's got too many connections. You better not try anything like that again."

Hazel shook her head slowly.

Aunt Sophie hummed. She cradled one hand in the other against her chest.

Janie gave Jason a little shove. "Get your toes out of the dirt and go fetch some iced tea."

He glanced down and saw that his feet were still rooted through the floor. "They don't want iced tea," he said, gathering more of himself and sternly talking it back into human shape.

"Too bad," said Janie. "That's what we got, so that's what we'll give 'em. Go on."

He grinned and wandered back to the kitchen. The glasses of iced tea were still where he had left them on the counter. He wondered if there was a chance the tea would still be cold and strong and the ice unmelted, but the possibility was very faint, so he emptied the glasses and refilled them, listening to the murmur of Janie's conversation with her family.

There was a very strong possibility that she would convince them to leave, and soon. He didn't actually grab that possibility until after he brought the tea out, though, and they all took some.

Toobychubbies

You know how it goes when you have two kids who are less than four years old. You view the advent of the Toobychubbies as a godsend, because no matter how good your intentions are to be the best mother in the universe, you have a finite amount of energy, and the kids are perpetual motion machines.

Actually, my kids are fraternal twins. Their names are Peter and Alice, and they're three and a half years old. On good days I think they look just like angels, and my heart fills so full of love for them it hurts.

I hadn't had a good day in a long time, though.

Peter lay on the floor, screaming, drumming his heels, and punching air. Tears streamed from his eyes. Alice hid in the corner with her hands clamped over her ears. When I saw her do that, I always wanted to do it myself, but I was supposed to be the mommy, so I didn't.

I didn't hear the doorbell until Peter stopped to catch his breath.

I tripped twice on trucks on my way through the living room and front hall, but managed to avoid getting more than a palm scrape. The blood from that matched a lot of the scribbling and grape jelly palm prints that were on the wall already. Treacherous loose pieces of giant Legos tried to get me, but I dodged them. I did step on a baby doll. Fortunately Peter's screams covered its bleated "Mama."

I flung open the door. My neighbor Barbara and her kids

stood on the front porch. Barbara said, "Again?" as Peter continued to scream and sob. Barbara's kids clutched her coat and half hid behind her.

"I'm so sorry," I said. I wanted to scream myself.

"Here." Barbara handed me a videotape with the word TOOBYCHUBBIES written on a label on its spine in black Sharpie. "Try this. Gotta run. Ruthie, Evie, be nice to Aunt Norma." She leaned down and detached her kids from her coat, kissed them, and shoved them toward me. She handed me their day bag, then ran down my front walk.

Ruth and Eve started crying. I couldn't hear them over Peter's rage, but I saw their tears and sniffles. I put down the day bag and the video and knelt beside them, hugging them. Gosh, I wished Barbara would take me away from all this too.

Little hot heads pressed against my shoulders. Small hands clutched at me. We sat in a huddle for a long time. Barbara drove off in her purple Neon. Eventually Peter ran out of screams. Eventually the girls resigned themselves to being abandoned. I still didn't want to move, but eventually I stood up, led the girls inside, and shut the front door.

I wiped their noses for them and patted the tears from their cheeks with Kleenex. Ruthie, who had just turned five, gave one final sniff, then picked up the video and handed it to me. She looked solemn. She usually did. Eve, three and a half, sucked on her index finger. "So," I said, "this show is something you like?"

Eve nodded and smiled.

Ruth made a face. "It's so baby," she said.

"Peter baby," Eve pointed out.

Ruth wrinkled her nose.

"Let's try it," I said. We went to the living room, Eve kicking aside trucks on the way with glee.

Peter lay pale and tear-damp on the rug. He had worn

himself out. Alice, in the corner, sat up but hugged her knees tight. I went straight to the TV/VCR complex and stuck the tape in. Eve and Ruth ran to the big couch and climbed up on it, then settled in the middle.

"Video?" Alice asked. She got to her feet and went to sit by Eve.

"Video," I said. It started playing automatically. I shut it off, leaving the TV with a blank blue screen, then grabbed the remote and picked up Peter. I sat next to Ruth on the couch, with Peter in my lap, and started the video again.

Tootly flute and spunky organ music, an idyllic landscape of gentle hills, grass and flowers and sky, a wandering camera eye that zoomed us over the hills and past rabbits and baby goats and sheep, then swooped over one last hill, and there sat a softly silver spaceship with blinking lights around its rim.

A ramp lowered with a whoosh. Out onto it ventured five brightly colored little creatures, totally plush velvet except their faces. They giggled and marched down the ramp, counting off as they lined up. "One! Two! Three! Four! Five!" Each one was a different size and color, but they all looked plump and cuddly: magenta; emerald green; sky blue; orange; lavender. Their faces ranged in flesh tones from pale to pink to yellow to brown. Each one had a pair of antennae reminiscent of "My Favorite Martian."

"Toobychubbies!" crooned a child's excited voice.

"Toobychubbies!" Ruth and Eve cried.

Peter, limp, hot, and heavy in my lap, straightened and stared.

"Toobychubbies," Alice repeated in a whisper voice, memorizing.

The little creatures giggled and laughed behind their hands, and then ran away, out of view, each in a different direction.

I blinked. How late had I been awake last night, anyway? It seemed like forever. Bob had wanted to discuss a problem at work long after lights out, and Peter kept calling from the twins' room that he needed another glass of water. Between them I'd been up until about three, I guessed, and then Alice had awakened me at six-thirty because she wanted her shoes.

I had hoped I could hold out until the afternoon, when I put the kids down for a nap and often took one myself, but right now I felt so sleepy.

I blinked again and opened my eyes. Time had passed. Now the smallest Toobychubby, Gita, the orange one, was inside the spaceship. I tried to focus. "Gita picks up toys," Gita said in a breathless and enchanting little voice.

"Gita picks up toys," repeated a deep voice. Gita looked up at a speaker grille on a stand, then nodded to it as though it could see her. She ran around picking up strangely shaped blocks from the Pepto-Bismol pink floor and putting them into a magic drawer that opened from the wall whenever she came near it. She had to search for the last couple of toys, which moved by themselves and played hide-and-seek with her, but she eventually tracked them down and put them away.

"Gita plays with toys!" she said when she had finished.

"Gita plays with toys!" said the male voice from the speaker.

Gita tapped the magic drawer and its sides dropped, spilling out all the toys she had just collected. Gita shrieked with glee and slid blocks across the smooth floor like hockey pucks, messing the sponge-walled room up again. The other Toobychubbies rushed in and helped her play with the toys.

What is this? I wondered. I yawned, then glanced at the children. All four stared at the screen, transfixed.

"Gita picks up toys," Gita said after the Toobychubbies

had played for a while, building towers and knocking them down.

"Gita picks up toys."

"Koko picks up toys," said the biggest Toobychubby.

"Wicky-wacky picks up toys."

"Bee picks up toys."

"Anashi picks up toys."

All the Toobychubbies picked up toys and put them away in the magic drawer.

"Bee plays with toys!" said Bee, and the drawer flopped open again, spilling all the toys out.

Honestly. How often could you watch the same scene over? I checked the children. Still rapt. I leaned back against the couch cushions.

The next thing I knew, Ruth shook me awake. "Aunt Norma? Can we have lunch now?"

Lunch! I looked at the clock. It was noon. Noon! I had slept for almost four hours! Frantic, I checked the children. What had they done while I was unconscious?

They still lined the couch like baby owls on a branch. Peter still sat in my lap.

So improbable! Peter was an active listener, had to be running all over while he watched a tape or listened to music. Eve was active too, usually jumping up and down and talking loudly to whatever was making noise. Ruth often retreated from stuff she thought was too babyish for her, finding some toy she considered more mature and playing with it not too far from the rest of us. A child marooned in the world of toddlers. I felt sorry for her, but Barbara and I had worked out this shared care system, and it was still better than any other plan we had come up with.

Quiet children. This was weird.

The tape had stopped. The kids all looked fine, if unnaturally still. Maybe they had been running around like hooligans the minute before; I couldn't tell.

I shook my head to get some awake into it. "Lunch. Of course. You're all okay?"

"We're fine, Aunt Norma," Ruth said. "We've been here all along."

"Oh. Great!" I wanted to kiss Ruth. She was such a great kid. How did Barbara get such a great kid?

"Who needs a diaper change?" I asked, setting Peter on his feet on the floor.

"I do," Peter said in a small voice.

"I do," Eve said.

"Let's do that first, then make lunch." I led them to the changing table and glanced at Alice, who was shy about this.

According to the child care books, all three of the little ones should be potty-trained by now, but somehow neither Barbara nor I had managed to work it out with the kids.

God, I hated changing diapers. But it was better than not changing them.

When I'd finished with Peter and Eve, I gave them toys and took Alice to the table. I set her on it and waited.

She looked down. "Change please," she whispered.

Afterward we all washed our hands and went into the kitchen. I got out Wonder bread and peanut butter and jelly.

"I hate peanut butter," Ruth said suddenly.

"No you don't," Eve said.

"Yes I do. It's sticky and yucky."

"Do you want a plain jelly sandwich?" I asked.

Mollified, Ruth nodded. Everybody else managed with pbj's and celery and carrot sticks.

"Did you like the show?" I asked Peter and Alice.

"Yes," both of them said.

After lunch we watched the tape again.

★ ★ ★ ★ ★

By the time Bob came home, I had had the equivalent of a full night's sleep. I didn't know if the children napped at all. They were all present and seemed healthy when I woke up and checked them just before Barbara arrived to pick up her two.

I felt like the ultimate bad parent. How could I fall asleep with awake babies in the house? What if something horrible had happened? I had child-proofed the house as soon as the twins could walk, but there was always something else you'd never imagine in a million years it would occur to them to put in their mouths. There was always something else they could break. There was always the chance they would figure out how to open a door, and a world of danger waited just outside.

They all knew they were supposed to ask me if they wanted to go anywhere, do anything, get something to eat, even try to use the potty. Mostly they *would* ask. Peter sometimes flew into passions where he forgot everything he knew, and acted without thought; Eve sometimes got distracted by events of the moment, and impulses overcame her.

When the darkest despairs dropped over me and I wondered why I should go on living, I had a hard time rousing to answer their questions, and they knew that. But this wasn't like that. I had only been asleep. They all knew how to wake me up.

"It's okay, Aunt Norma," Ruth assured me. She patted my shoulder. "We're fine."

Aside from the load of guilt that had avalanched me, I felt refreshed. I glanced at the clock and packed up Ruth's and Eve's day bag. "Did you get enough to eat?" I asked. "I must have slept through snack time."

"We had Cheerios," Ruth said, shaking a plastic container

from the day bag. A few Cheerios rattled around inside it.

"I didn't mean to sleep."

"S'okay, Mama." Peter gave me a heart-melting smile.

"S'okay," Alice echoed.

The doorbell rang, and Barbara breezed in. "Nice day?" she asked, smiling at the quiet children. "Let's go!"

I popped the tape out of the VCR. It had rewound itself, so the kids must have watched it all the way to the end, where auto-rewind kicked in. "How long is this, anyway?"

"Eight episodes. What did you think?"

I couldn't tell her I had slept through it. "The kids thought it was great. We watched it twice."

"Whoa," she said. "We usually just do one episode at a time."

"Well . . ." How could she stop after one episode? Maybe it didn't put *her* to sleep.

I held the tape out to her, but she said, "You keep it. You can use it again tomorrow."

"Sure," I said. *No way,* I thought.

Ruth and Eve said good-bye to Alice and Peter. As soon as Barbara and her kids were out the door, I looked around. "Time to clean up," I said.

Peter crowed with laughter. After a minute, Alice laughed too. Her laugh was rusty and faint from disuse. Even if they were laughing at me, I thought, it was good to hear it.

I frowned at the carpet. Not a toy in sight. What about the myriad trucks and blocks and small doll parts I'd been tripping over that morning?

"Peter picks up toys," said Peter. He pointed to the toy bin.

"Alice picks up toys."

Sure enough, the toy bin held heaps of toys, and the carpet held none. "Wow," I said. "You guys are like brownies.

Wanna help me make dinner?"

We all went to the kitchen and worked on dinner. Toobychubbies. Gotta love 'em.

The next morning was another nightmare in the series. Peter threw oatmeal all over the kitchen when I wouldn't give him an extra spoonful of brown sugar on it. Alice disappeared, and I hadn't located her by the time Barbara arrived. I was going crazy trying to find her. Peter stood in the kitchen with a half-eaten piece of toast and screamed. On a ten-to-one scale of tantrum-level screams, these were only about a seven, but they made me want to hide somewhere too.

"Again?" Barbara said when I opened the door to her.

"I can't find Alice!"

"She's not out here," Barbara said. "Is the kitchen door locked?"

"Locked and chained."

"She's got to be somewhere in the house." She draped the day bag over my shoulder, shoved Ruth and Eve into the house, said, "Gotta run. Bye, kids. See you later," and ran to her car.

I couldn't spare Eve and Ruth much of a hug that morning. I had to find Alice before something awful happened to her. So they cried, and I felt miserable. "Help me look for Alice," I said. We could tell where Peter was. His screams had slowed to intermittent and quieted to conversational, but they still came strongly from the kitchen.

We checked everywhere sensible. Ruth jiggled doorknobs to closed closets. "Look here," she said.

"But there's no way she could have gotten in there. I always keep that door closed."

"Look here."

Alice was hiding in the linen closet. It was the third closet we checked. How did she get in there? "Come on, sweetie," I said, lifting her out from the nest she had made among the blankets. Her face was stony and still, and she held herself rigid in my arms, not softening at all.

In the end I put the tape in again, but this time I left the room. "Call me if you need anything. I'll be in the kitchen," I said.

"We will," said Ruth.

So I sorted laundry and loaded it into the machine, cleaned up from breakfast, scrubbed down kitchen walls that bore three months' worth of tossed-food mural, read a mystery novel, and every fifteen minutes or so I checked on the children. Toobychubbies completely enraptured them. I couldn't look at the screen for more than twenty seconds without feeling sleepy, though.

At ten I remote-controlled the tape off. "Snacks," I said, offering apple sections and peanut-butter crackers and water in sippy cups. They all came willingly enough, smiling, not talking, and definitely not screaming.

I tried to interest them in a walk to the park, but that started Peter screaming again. "Toobychubbies!" he yelled. Eve cried. Alice looked stormy. Ruth shrugged a lot.

It couldn't be good for them to spend a whole day watching TV.

I turned the tape on again after snacks, though.

After lunch I tried to get them to go outside, but no.

"I don't know about this," I told Barbara when she came to pick up her kids. "They watched it all day. I couldn't get them away from it. Maybe you should take it home and keep it there."

"I bought the next tape," she said, and smiled. "I subscribed to the series. There's a new tape every month with eight episodes on it."

"But—" What about exercise? What about play? What, exactly, were these tapes putting into our children's minds?

"They have the *Good Housekeeping* seal of approval. They're recommended by *Parents Magazine*. Come on, Norma, admit it. These things work."

"Work at what?"

The next day was Friday, Barbara's day to take my kids. I spent the day not working on my art, which was what I did most Fridays; unlike Barbara, I didn't have an actual outside job. I took her kids four days a week, and she took my kids one, and we set up the weekends to suit our schedules. Barbara gave me two dollars an hour to watch her kids, with eight free hours of child care from me in exchange for the one day she watched my kids, which gave me an income of about fifty dollars a week. I spent the money on paints and colored pencils and sketch pads, mostly. Then I sat around at the kitchen table on Friday with my art supplies and tried to make a mark, any mark, on a blank page.

What was the matter with me? In college I'd been able to mess up reams of paper without thinking twice. Somehow now I was afraid to even start. What if it wasn't perfect? What if I wrinkled a page? What if I chose the wrong color? The wrong subject?

That day I actually did a colored pencil sketch of a bowl of apples. It was awful. I was deep in the miseries by the time Barbara brought Alice and Peter home.

That day they didn't hang onto her coat hem and beg her to take them home with her again. She kissed them and sent them in to me, dropped the day bag on the floor, waved, and dashed out the door.

"You have a good day?" I asked my kids.

"Grrrreat," Peter said.

"Toobychubbies," said Alice. She wandered over and picked up two wadded pieces of paper. She threw them out, then moved to the table, where she climbed up on a chair and straightened my pencils. Peter saw what she was doing and joined her.

Sunk into despair, I sat and watched my children sort my pencils by color. Alice arranged them in a proper spectrum. Peter watched, then switched them around so they were in a reverse spectrum. They both stared at the pencils, then laughed and did it again.

I became accustomed to napping on the couch while the children sat around the television, staring at brightly colored aliens who crooned, giggled, made messes, and then cleaned them up. Ruth took charge of the remote control. She stopped the show when it was time for snacks, and woke me up to fix them. She stopped the show if anybody needed me for anything. I relaxed into this new system, smothering my doubts.

I knew I shouldn't let a child mother me and the others. She was too young for this kind of responsibility. But she seemed contented with it.

So maybe the kids weren't so energetic anymore. They fussed a lot less. Peter screamed a lot less, and Alice no longer spent so much time hiding. We all slept through the night more often, and when I did get the kids to go shopping or to the park, they weren't always trying to run off, scream at strangers, or hit each other.

Bob even stopped complaining about work so much. Our sex life shifted, too. I kept him happy without actually participating much myself; I used my hand. Afterward I felt good, he seemed ecstatic, and we both slept better.

The children cooperated with each other, built block

towers together without knocking each other's work over, broke jobs into chunks and each took a piece. They helped me with everything. If I emptied the dishwasher, for example, one would put away forks, one spoons, one knives, one bowls. They were eerie but efficient, and they kept quiet most of the time.

Having the Toobychubby theme song play in my head at all hours of the night and day seemed like a small price to pay for model children.

I did notice that most of the mothers I bumped into at the supermarket or in the toy store or at the video rental store were, well, humming. We caught ourselves singing along with each other.

Then the whispers started.

I heard them best when I was already depressed and half asleep on the couch. "Stay small. Stay cute. Eat less. Say less. Be good. Be good. Be good. Help more. Stay small . . ."

Food stopped tasting so good. A week's worth of groceries stretched to two weeks' worth; we liked eating off smaller plates. I could stand to lose a few pounds—who couldn't?

Well, Alice, for one. She had always been a picky eater. Now she was way too skinny. I took her in for a checkup, but the doctor said she was fine.

We're all fine, I thought. *Stay small. Stay cute. Eat less. Feel good. Hug!*

"Do you ever find yourself falling asleep during the tapes?" I asked Barbara one summer Sunday when she and her husband Al and Bob and I were at the lake, watching the children on the beach. Barbara and I had slathered sun-block on the children and each other. I loved the feel of the sun beating down on my back; it drove the dank miseries back a bit.

Bob and Al, their legs hairy and white, backs pale from

business-suited days, danced in the water's edge with the children.

"I can't stand those tapes," Barbara said in a low voice. "They totally creep me out, but the kids love them. What can you do? I just leave the room, but I keep an eye on the kids. Have you noticed they never fight anymore?"

"Yeah," I said. "But . . . don't you hear the . . . well, the . . . whispers?"

"What are you talking about, Norma? Say, you're looking good. That swimsuit is way too big on you. You need a new one. What kind of diet are you on?"

"They're not growing," I said. "The kids. They're not getting bigger."

"Dr. Klossner said Ruthie and Evie are fine." An edge of fear touched her voice.

So maybe I hadn't been imagining it all.

"So their development is a little delayed," Barbara said. "It happens with some kids."

I looked down the beach. Mothers and fathers and children lay on towels, or waded in the summer-warm water. All the kids looked so . . . cute. And small. They giggled behind their hands. Nobody screamed bloody murder or hit anyone else. Nobody played tug-of-war with a toy boat or a bucket. Lots and lots of the kids hugged plush toy Toobychubbies.

"Don't you think—" I began.

"Just shut up about it. It's easier now." She laid her head on her towel, her face turned away from me. She whispered, so soft I almost didn't hear it, "They used to cry when I left. It broke my heart every morning."

Heat relaxed me. "Do you like it better now?" I asked after a long piece of time had slipped by.

She didn't answer right away. I thought she might have fallen asleep. At last she said, "No."

★ ★ ★ ★ ★

"But we *have* to see the tape, Aunt Norma," Ruth told me.

"Today we're going to the Natural History Museum. You'll like it. Remember all the birds' nests with eggs in them? How about the raccoons?"

"Tape first. Then we can go out," Ruth said. She sounded so confident and in charge I almost gave way.

"Trip first. Then tape."

Ruth looked at Alice, Peter, and Eve. Solemn, skinny, good-looking kids, all of them, with an air of gravity that sat oddly on their four-year-old shoulders. Alice shrugged.

"Okay," said Ruth, in a just-this-once tone.

I took my sketch pad.

I have one perfect picture from that day, the day before the aliens landed and we all supposedly learned what the Toobychubbies had been teaching our children and why. It shows my children and Barbara's, tiny black silhouettes, standing in front of the life-size cement Apatosaurus that's out in front of the museum. There is nothing of movement or excitement about those toddler-sized silhouettes face to face with something vast and ancient; only contemplation, a kind of waiting.

Bob doesn't understand why I framed that picture and hung it in the upstairs hall. But then, he doesn't understand much about our current situation. Worldwide, scientists are still wild with excitement because of their daily discoveries concerning the aliens. I've seen newscasts and talk shows praising the aliens: how they have created a whole generation of children with coping skills that don't involve aggression, children who know how to love each other and cooperate with each other. What a future we will have because of this wonderful alien intervention!

They haven't heard the whispers, which I guess can't be there. Since the landing, the Toobychubbies shows have been exhaustively analyzed for subliminal content, and nobody's mentioned the whispers. Child development specialists still aren't sure why the show has the effect it has.

The whispers said, *Stay small. Eat less. Play fair. Stay cute. Be good. No sex.*

I know, if no one else does, what our children have been trained to be: our last generation.

Sometimes I hug them a little too hard, but they never complain.

Haunted Humans

1

Dorothy Jean Demain, presently known as Dorothy Jean Hand, sometimes called Dot by people who didn't know her and almost always D.J. by those who did, gripped the phone handset between her ear and shoulder. Her right hand held a pen poised over a carbonless message pad; her left hand sorted the Mental Healing Center's mail. The four office hours following Friday's lunch break stretched ahead, aggravated by dealing with the operator who had picked up when D.J. rang the answering service.

"Sandy, have you checked account 551 for me yet?" D.J. said as patiently as she could, breaking in on two minutes of inane chatter.

She listened to Sandy splutter through a message for Dr. Arlene Bollings, D.J.'s boss, managing to extract relevant information with great difficulty. She was just about to demand the phone number of the person leaving the message when Sandy broke in with, "Uh, but—hey, Dot, there's a message here for you, too."

"Let's finish with the first one, please." D.J. could hear her voice tightening. She wanted to grab Sandy and shake the information out of her like salt. But she was in secretary mode right now, level, efficient, no matter what the circumstances.

She hunched her shoulders, then took a calming breath.

"But the one for you is creepy." Sandy's voice was high, her words slow. D.J. wondered what she looked like; all she could tell was that Sandy chewed gum loudly and snappingly, and occasionally smoked; the small sucked intakes of breath were a giveaway.

"I still need the phone number on this one, Sandy." Sandy had purged vital information from the files without communicating it before. D.J. had learned the hard way to persist with her.

After three tries, Sandy managed to tell her the phone number. D.J. wrote, sighed, and said, "Is that it for this message?"

"Yeah, I guess. There's one from that psycho nutcase Dr. Kabukin's seeing—"

D.J. resisted an urge to ask just which psycho nutcase. Dr. Kabukin handled therapy cases, while Dr. Bollings did divorce, custody, and criminal evaluations for the courts. D.J. generally liked Dr. Kabukin's patients better. Most of them were interested in changing. Most of Dr. Bollings's patients were interested in fooling the doctor.

"—a couple real boring messages for the other doctors, and then this one for you. It's pretty weird, Dot."

"Why don't you read it to me?" *And get it over with?* D.J. poised her pen at the top of the next message blank, wondering if Sandy would communicate any of the information in order.

"To, uh, Dorothy Jean, from Chase. Do you suppose that's a first or a last name?"

To stop her hand from shaking, D.J. pressed the pen down on the message form so hard it punched through several sheets. "Go on."

"There's, like, no number. It just says, 'You know what I

need and I'm coming to get it.' Don't you think that's weird?"

D.J. said nothing.

"Well, I do. Kind of creepy. Did you get that? 'You know what I need and I'm coming to get it.' Dot, you still there? Darn, I bet she hung up. Why do people always hang up on me?"

Deciding to take this as a suggestion, D.J. quietly lowered the phone's handset until it clicked into the cradle. Chase? It couldn't be Chase. She stared over the four-foot-high divider that separated her desk and computer hutch from the office waiting room, her gaze finally settling on the crystal vase of Double Delight roses Dr. Kabukin had brought in that morning and set among the magazines and self-help books on the glass-topped table between the two blue-and-white striped couches. Look how pink and white the roses are, D.J. thought, just like a baby, perhaps, or the hopes of a young girl on her wedding night.

From the white walls, colorful abstract pictures glowed in the sun slanting through the picture window. Leftover Oregon raindrops glistened on the lawn out front. Everything in D.J.'s view looked cool and clean and calm. Untouched tranquility, like her life before Chase.

She shuddered and lifted the phone again. For a moment she closed her eyes tight, concentrating on crushing all the thoughts she didn't want to entertain. She pressed autodial for the answering service, and smiled down at the message pad when Poppy picked up.

"Account 551, please," D.J. said, and took the rest of the messages without a hitch.

Morgan Hesch sat on one of the puffy striped couches in the Mental Healing Center waiting room and stared at the bits of dirt he'd tracked on the white speckled rug. Why did they have a lawn out front if they wanted to keep the rug clean? Well, yeah, there was a brick walk that wound across the lawn, but what if you were coming from the other direction? And the lawn was green and healthy, but there were those flower beds. Somebody must rake the edges all the time to make the dirt look so—so *clean*. Like nothing had ever stepped on it since the dawn of time. Morgan hated that kind of clean. If blackboards were bare in his college classes when he got there, he always chalked something on them before he sat down. If the dirt were blank, he just had to put a footprint in it. If things were wide open, any force, good or evil, could enter and control them.

So the floor was no longer blank, either, not peppered with those chunks of earth that had fallen out of the waffle-stomper soles of his hiking boots. Morgan looked at the bits of squared dirt and slid his left hand in between the third and fourth buttons on his shirt, hiding it against his chest. One of his insiders, Shadow, always wanted to hide Morgan's hands.

"Miss Deej?" Morgan said, his knees knocking against each other, not because he was cold, just to be doing something.

He could only see the top of her head over the wall that hid the desk from him and everybody else. She had messy frizzy brown hair that she parted in the middle. He watched the part lean back until he could see Deej's eyes, green like the devil's, over the divider as she looked at him.

"Yes, Morgan," she said. One of her better voices. Not the first-time-&-phone voice which said, I'm-here-to-help,-don't-bother-to-know-I'm-human. Definitely not the I-can't-have-a-relationship-with-you-because-it-wouldn't-be-professional voice. She'd given up on that one after he'd been seeing Dr. Dara Kabukin for two months. Not the don't-bother-me-I'm-in-the-middle-of-something voice, and not the okay-okay-

139

yes-I-guess-I-can-look-up voice. More of a I-don't-know-what-I'm-doing-but-I'm-glad-for-a-distraction voice. Actually he didn't think he'd ever heard her use this one before.

Morgan figured Deej must have insiders since she had lots of voices like he did. Also, she was one of the few people who could recognize his insiders just by the way they talked. Even Dr. Dara got confused sometimes, but Deej always knew who was talking if it was anybody she'd ever talked to before. Timmy liked to play tricks on Deej, but even he was happy when the tricks didn't work. Morgan wondered if Deej had ever thought about being a doctor. Even though her hair was messy and she had the devil's eyes, he might go see her if she were a doctor.

"I'm thirsty," he said.

"Would you like some water?"

"Yes, please. And paper? Pencil?" The voice that asked the last part belonged to the newest insider, who wasn't used to using Morgan's vocal cords and wasn't supposed to talk until Morgan had gotten to know him, anyway. The new insider's voice hadn't sorted itself out yet; it sounded a lot like Morgan.

Deej stood up so he could see about a third of her, the top third. She was wearing a blue and white shirt, and some little bits of color on her lips, just the outside edges. Mostly if she had any color on her lips, it was all over them.

Today was not like other days.

She held out some white paper and a pencil with a blunt tip. After he took the things from her, she headed into the other room, the one with the sink and the little baby fridge and the table where you took tests.

The new insider was clamoring to get its hands on the paper and pencil. Morgan's appointment with Dr. Dara wouldn't start for another fifteen minutes. Morgan asked this anxious new insider if fifteen minutes would be enough, and the insider said he'd do what he could, if it was okay with Morgan. Sure, said Morgan. He sat back and let go of his hands. The insider used the left hand to draw a picture real fast of a man's face. The man had dark thick eyebrows and shadowy eyes and his mouth was wide but it sure wasn't smiling. What interested Morgan as he watched the picture form in front of him was that it looked like a photograph, with gray places under the nose and eyebrows, like parts of the face stuck right out of the paper and had shadows. He had never drawn anything like this before.

He finished. Deej brought him a cup with water in it, then looked at his picture without asking and dropped the water. The water splashed on Deej's sandals. Some hit Morgan's hiking boots, but most of it hit the rug.

"Miss Deej," said Morgan.

"Ah, ah, ah, oh, I'm sorry, Morgan," she said, breathing like a dog on a hot day. "I'll get you another."

"Miss Deej, you having a seizure?" he asked.

"Well, maybe, yes, maybe," she said, and ran into the sink-fridge-test room.

Today was definitely not like other days. Morgan had never seen Deej upset before.

When she came back, she handed him the water without spilling any and said, "Morgan, who is that a picture of?"

"I don't know. One of the insiders did it."

"Which insider?"

"Now, Miss Deej," said Clift, "you know it would be unprofessional of us to discuss our case with the secretary."

"Oh, come on, Clift," said Deej. "I'm not asking you for a diagnosis or even intimate personal details. I was just wondering which one of you did it."

Clift thought that over, and said, "Well, the truth is, Miss

Deej, we can't tell you which insider. Somebody new is all we know."

"Do you know who the man in the picture is?"

"Do you?" asked Mishka in her little baby girl voice. She thought it was a game. She was three and thought most things were games.

"Do *you*?" Deej repeated.

"I asked you first," said Mishka.

"I asked you second, and two is bigger than one."

"Well, *I* don't know," Mishka said, but at the same time the left hand was writing something on the piece of paper. Morgan looked down. "Chase Kennedy," the words said.

Deej put her hands over her mouth. Her eyes got wide.

"Somebody you know?" Saul asked, with an ugly edge to his tone. Saul was mean to everybody. Morgan didn't like it when Saul took the voice because he made people not like Morgan.

"Somebody you know?" Deej said, right back. She'd met Saul before and she still liked Morgan. One of the few.

"No," said Saul.

"How could you draw a picture of somebody you don't know? Did you see his picture in a magazine or something?"

"There are some things mankind was not meant to know," said the Shadow in his creepy echoey voice.

"How about womankind?" asked Deej, but just then the phone rang and she disappeared back behind her desk. Her voice turned into the polite-to-company voice she always used on the phone as she said, "Good afternoon, Mental Healing Center, may I help you?"

Dr. Dara came out of the door to the back hallway, smiling and leading a young fat woman toward the door to outside. "All right, Elena, same time next week?" she said, her voice faintly accented. Only two of the insiders had accents that

Morgan could hear, and they were Valerie, the Southern one, and Saul, who was from New Jersey. The rest of his insiders sounded pretty much like people on TV. Dr. Dara was from somewhere else. England? England, even though she had narrow black eyes and totally black hair like people from Japan.

The fat woman stared at the floor, mumbled something, glanced up quickly at Dr. Dara and then away again. Morgan remembered being like that when he first started seeing the doctor, not being able to look anybody in the eye, not being able to talk clearly, not wanting anybody to look at him. When the insiders had first come, they made him do things and he was in trouble all the time because of them and he couldn't get them to cooperate. Even though it was his body, they didn't listen to him. Not till Clift came, and started getting everybody to work as a team. Morgan studied the patient. She wore a big ugly navy-blue dress, and a belt that cut into her middle, and her hair was heavy and tangled, her face greasy, with little sores on it.

Mishka felt sorry for her and said, "Bye bye. Bye bye."

The fat woman looked at him like she was scared, which probably wasn't what Mishka meant to happen. Mishka wasn't very good at figuring out how people would feel about what she did. The others tried to talk her out of taking control without asking, but she had these impulses all the time and you couldn't watch out for them twenty-six hours a day. Morgan shrugged. "Sorry," he said. Then he gave speech number six, one Dr. Dara had drilled him on for several weeks: "Didn't mean anything by it. Have a nice day."

"Thanks," said the fat woman, trying to smile and frowning instead.

"Take care, Elena," Dr. Dara said, escorting her out the

door. She sighed as she shut the door behind the woman, then turned. Every hair was in place—Clift sometimes called Dr. Dara "Helmet-head"—and her lipstick was bright and even. She smiled. "Morgan," she said.

"She's a new one, right?"

"Absolutely new. You were very good, Morgan. Come on back to the office. What have you drawn today? Who did it?"

"It's a picture for Miss Deej," Morgan said. "A guy named Campbell did it."

Deej stared at him.

"He just told me, Deej. I didn't know before, honest. Gary Campbell."

"Gary?" said Deej, her voice high and little like Mishka's. Definitely Morgan and Deej had something in common. Morgan wondered what she would say if he asked her for a date. He had the impression that people in the office weren't supposed to date patients.

The new insider, Gary, was trying to get a word out. Morgan thought that was pretty pushy for somebody who'd just come to him, so he and Clift squashed the guy down. "Wait your turn, Gary," Morgan said, but he handed the picture to Deej.

"Thanks," she said, still in that little high voice.

"I like you, Miss Deej," Morgan said, figuring that would be something she'd remember he had said until he finished talking to Dr. Dara, and then he might ask Deej about the date idea.

"Come on, Morgan," said Dr. Dara.

As Morgan followed Dr. Dara back into her office, Clift came out. "Let's not discuss integration today, Doctor, all right? You know we're not a true multiple, and I think integration would be bad for Morgan. If anything, he needs to build himself up at the expense of the rest of us. He's still too wide open. Imagine us picking up another one. I can't seem to convince him to close the door. You get him started thinking he can work us in here with him and he'll start accepting any damn Tom, Dick, or Mary that comes along and knocks."

"What topic would you suggest, Clift?" asked Dr. Dara.

"We definitely, definitely, need more work on socialization. That speech worked—wasn't that great? We've said that about six times in the correct context since last week, and Morgan's finally starting to believe it works. I tell him things and tell him things and he just doesn't pay attention, but when you tell him, he actually listens."

"Well, yes, that is my function, Clift. Let me just check with Morgan, see if he's got an agenda for this afternoon, all right?"

"Okay," said Clift grumpily and subsided.

"Did you find the tape in the Dictaphone?" Dr. Bollings asked D.J. as D.J. handed her a stack of message slips and opened and sorted mail.

"Oh," D.J. said. With the picture Morgan had drawn in front of her, she had had trouble concentrating on work at all. She turned the picture face down and forced all her thoughts about Chase away. She had had a lot of practice ditching thoughts of Chase, but she knew she would have to think hard about him soon. This was just too weird. Something must have happened. She needed to find and read some recent newspapers, though she had been avoiding news in the three years since the trial. "It's been such a madhouse I haven't gone into your office since lunchtime. Is the tape long? I'll stay till I finish typing it."

"Just a few letters, but they should go out today."

"I'll get right on it." She got the tape out of Dr. Bollings's Dictaphone, plugged it into her own, rewound it, started the computer, macro'd up the letter format, and began typing, putting her brain on auto.

Dear Dr. Kennedy:
    I was pleased to receive your recent inquiry regarding office space. Regrettably, I must tell you that our last vacancy was filled a month ago. If I can be of any help to you in recommending other local office facilities, please do not hesitate to contact me.

Sincerely,
Arlene Bollings, Ph.D.

The tape went on: "Oh, D.J., would you look up that address? It's on the envelope in the out basket."

Damn, thought D.J., *I was in such a hurry to get the tape I forgot to check the out basket.* Just then Dr. Bollings came out of her office with a handful of papers and gave them to D.J.

"Thanks, Boss," D.J. said and sighed.

"You're in some kind of mood today, aren't you?" asked Dr. Bollings.

"What was your first clue?"

The doctor just smiled. "Lucky the schedule's light today. Rest up over the weekend. I've got five reports to dictate, and I plan to spend a lot of Saturday over a hot mike, so you'll have plenty to do on Monday."

"Promises, promises," said D.J. She sorted through the stack of papers, and found the letter and envelope from Dr. Kennedy on the bottom of the pile.

D.J. put the letter on the copystand next to her keyboard and positioned the cursor a line below the date so she could type in the address.

Dr. Chase Kennedy, Ph.D.

"Arlene!" D.J. cried.

2

D.J.'s landlady Afra was watering the dwarf dahlias in the front planter at the Coat of Arms Apartments building when D.J. parked her six-year-old silver Tercel in the car port. D.J. groaned before she climbed out of the car and locked the door. Afra always wanted to talk, and D.J. was definitely not in the mood today.

"You got plans for the weekend, hon, or you going to spend it holed up with the TV again like the last six weeks? Have you thought about getting some sun? You're so pasty!" Afra said as D.J. trudged up the concrete walk toward the front door.

"Have you heard about UV?" D.J. said, then really wondered. Afra was who knew how old; her face was leathery and worn like any skin tanned by years of sunlight.

"UV? Is that short for some new kind of perversion or drug? I have trouble keeping up with the kinds of mischief you youngsters get into anymore."

"Uh, no, it's ultra-violet rays from the sun. They cause cancer."

"Doesn't everything," Afra said.

Before she could get started on another topic, D.J. said, "I've got to get inside and make dinner. I'm tired."

" 'Course you are, not enough fresh air, too much television, and improper nutrition." Afra waved her hand in a shooing motion. D.J. escaped. She checked her mailbox, afraid. She'd signed up here as D. J. Hand, and had paid to keep her number unlisted. But if Chase could track her to her job, he could track her to her home.

The only thing in her mailbox was the fall catalog for Community Education. She carried it upstairs to her second floor apartment, feeling relieved when she had fastened the chain from the inside.

Then she turned around to face her studio apartment and saw the writing on the wall. Red spray paint, right across her Van Gogh and Rembrandt art prints. "Only you can purify me. Only through your blood will I be saved."

She would never forget his handwriting.

She had seen it in the love notes he'd left with flowers, when he had courted her four years ago. Later, she had seen his handwriting on the anonymous notes that the police found next to the corpses. She had seen it in the letters Chase wrote her from Death Row.

Those letters had finally driven her to give up a paralegal position with a future in it at one of the big law firms in San Francisco and move north, to Spores Ferry, Oregon, a town of a hundred thousand, as small a place as she could live in and not go crazy, she figured. Gary Campbell, the first detective who had seriously listened to her when she mentioned her suspicions about her boyfriend to the task force, the one she had kept in contact with after the sentencing hearing, had told her she didn't even have to open the letters. Chase couldn't get her, he said. But she opened the letters. She had to. Finally she had run anyway. She hadn't left any forwarding address anywhere, not even with her mother.

And maybe she had been right, and Gary had been wrong. Maybe Chase had been playing with her, through the trial, the sentencing hearing, even his going to jail for three years, just so he could come back and find her now, hidden as she was, ferreting out her job and her apartment and everything she had to cling to in her new existence.

A knock sounded on her door. She jerked and gasped, dropping her mail and her purse. Her heart speeded. She looked around for anything she could use as a weapon, grabbed an antique umbrella she had picked up at a yard sale, and went to the door.

Through the peep she saw Morgan's gaunt young face, his wispy black mustache. He had done something to his hair; instead of hanging lank and half over his face, it had height to it. Mousse? Gel? Morgan with fashion sense? A frightening thought. And he was standing up straight. Usually she saw him slouched on a couch. He was taller than she had thought.

"You alone?" she asked through the door.

"Deej, you know me better than that."

She slipped the chain off and turned the locks. "I just got home," she said. "I wasn't expecting you for another hour."

"Would you like me to go away for a while?" asked his fruitiest and most refined voice.

"No, Clift; I was just explaining why I haven't had time to change. Actually, I'd like you to come in."

Morgan blinked and stared.

"Actually, I'm kind of scared right now." Her voice wobbled. She reached out and took his narrow hand, pulled him into the apartment. "Look." She pointed to the graffiti.

"Messy," said Morgan in an approving voice.

She looked sideways at him, this gawky college boy with his many voices, and thought, what a thin reed I'm leaning on. I should send him home and talk to the police. Tell them my history, ask them to find out whether Chase is still in jail or not. "Morgan, did you really ask Dr. Kabukin if it was all right for us to see each other?"

"No," he said.

"What? But you said—"

"Sure," said Saul. "She would have told me to forget it, so

I decided not to ask her. What do you think, lady, it's productive for a psycho to date his doctor's secretary? Jeeze, take a minute to think."

"Wait a second. I'm not the doctor around here. How would I know? Besides, you lied to me."

"Like no one's ever done that before?" Saul said, sneering.

"Morgan never did before," said D.J.

"How would you know?" Saul said.

"Shut up, Saul," said Clift. "D.J.'s right. Morgan never lied to her before. Of course, this particular lie was hopelessly transparent. Why did you believe it? You could have checked with Dr. Dara before you said yes to us. Usually you're so efficient."

"I—"

"I doubt it's the body," Clift continued, holding out his arms and looking down at Morgan's slender frame. "I've been trying to get him interested in swimming, but one of the others died by drowning and won't go near water. Or is this a body type that appeals to you?"

"No, I—"

"Wait a minute," Clift said. "Wait. A. Minute. It's Gary, isn't it?"

D.J. sighed and closed her eyes.

"That prick?" Saul yelled. "You know he's a cop? We got a damned cop in here with us. Pushy rude bastard!"

"D.J., is that the story? It's Gary you want to see?" Clift asked. "Was the picture that important?"

"I'm sorry, Clift. Sorry, Morgan. I think I know . . ." She couldn't believe what she was about to say. D.J. had never known quite what to make of Morgan and his many voices. Dr. Kabukin was not a slave to the *Diagnostic and Statistical Manual of Mental Disorders* the way Dr. Bollings was; she didn't diagnose her patients with number codes you could look up to identify their particular disorder. So D.J. didn't have a convenient label for Morgan. She just thought he was funny, and found several of his voices willing to play games with her, even though they also enjoyed irritating her.

But Gary—that was a different story. If Gary were Gary Campbell, the cop she had known in San Francisco . . . How could she deny it? How could Morgan possibly know enough about her to draw a picture of Chase Kennedy out of the blue? The explanation she came up with was too silly to think about. But she had to think about it anyway. Maybe all the voices in Morgan were indeed different people. Maybe he was psychic and tuned in to all these other people, or maybe —

"Clift, are you a ghost?"

"Why, D.J., you're the first person besides Morgan to come up with that explanation. I'm flattered."

"Yes, but would you answer?"

"And I've told Dr. Kabukin about that, too, but she continues to nurse her own pet theories. We do make progress, when she gives us ideas about how to handle society in a way that won't scare it, but when she tries to get us to consider getting together, one has to shudder."

D.J. tried a different tack. "How did you die, Clift?"

"In a ridiculously mundane fashion. A car crash. I had always hoped that I would irritate some rival intellectual into committing a fiendishly clever murder, but I didn't live long enough to achieve maximum irritation and my dream death. No, instead I was out driving to the university library one night when a drunk in a big American car crossed the center line and plowed right into the side of my small Japanese car, crushing it and me between his grill and the wall of a bank. A savings and loan, if I recall correctly. At least there was a metaphor there."

"What year was this?"

"Two years ago."

"Where?"

"East Lansing. They're very into big American cars there. Did you know that a number of car makers have factories there?"

"No," said D.J. "So how did you find Morgan?"

"Well, I was frustrated about suffering such a meaningless death, so I didn't feel ready to shuffle off this mortal coil. On the other hand, haunting a sidewalk or an auto junkyard didn't fulfill my need for some kind of recognition either. I was drifting around aimlessly, trying to figure out what I *could* do in my powerless state when I felt this peculiar pull from the west, and thought what the hell. I gave in and found myself sucked right into Morgan's body. He was playing with an *Ouija* board at the time. Since I arrived I've tried to discourage him from engaging in this game, but he's not always amenable to direction. Worse, he doesn't seem to need the board anymore; random spirits just show up here and crowd in with the rest of us."

D.J. bit her lower lip. She had found Clift the most reasonable of Morgan's voices, but just now she didn't know what to believe.

"But, to bring us up to speed, we were talking about Gary, weren't we?" Clift said.

She swallowed, and said, "I think I know Gary from when he was alive."

"Really? I thought that was just an attention-getting device on his part, claiming he had something to tell you. When we get somebody new we usually try to gentle them down for a while before we let them play with the body. They can get us in a lot of trouble if we let them out unsupervised. When Saul first came, Morgan woke up in a bordello across a state line, and went into shock. He's never quite recovered from the mortification. He's awfully young, something Saul refuses to take into consideration. But if Gary was telling the truth . . . May we sit down?"

"What? Oh, sure, sure," said D.J., clearing a stack of books off a chair for him. She closed and locked the door, then said, "Would you like something to drink? I've got instant coffee or tea or lemonade."

"No, thanks," said Clift. "We need a little quiet to thrash this out amongst ourselves. Excuse me, please."

"Sure," said D.J. She went into the kitchen and poured herself a nip of brandy, swallowed it without tasting. She coughed as the warmth bit into her, then decided to put some water in the kettle for tea anyway.

She was leaning on the counter, staring at the kettle and wondering if it would boil as she watched, when a new voice called to her from the living room/bed room/dining room. "Doro?"

She straightened, gripping her elbows so hard she could feel her fingertips drilling into her skin. After a moment and a couple of deep breaths she walked out into the living room and looked at Morgan.

His eyes, usually a pale blue, looked darker, and his mouth wore a crooked smile she had never seen there before, but she had seen it. She had seen it.

"Ain't this a bitch?" he said, and laughed, deep and low.

"Gary," she whispered, chilled.

"Poor bastard, lonely kid, just wants to make some friends, doesn't know how to talk to girls, invites in the wide world of spirits. Christ, Doro, never thought I'd see you again this way."

"Gary," she said, clutching her elbows, her shoulders hunching higher.

153

"Yes, well," he said, and tilted his head in a certain way, so that he was looking up at her from under his brows, "the world being as it is—Christ, Doro, what a world!—I think we should talk about the case again."

"Gary, how did you die?"

"That's the point, isn't it? Chase has escaped."

D.J. let out a scream just for the hell of it, releasing tension, then said, "Well, I kind of thought—" and pointed to the writing on the wall. "And he left messages for me at the office."

Gary looked up and his eyes went wide. "God, Doro! Get out of here!"

"Without a game plan? Let's think this through first."

"He knows where you live! Go somewhere else immediately."

"Oh, come on. I don't want to run around like a headless chicken. Let me pack a few things, and get my credit card and my bank numbers and like that."

"All those things can be traced. Ditch them."

"That doesn't make any sense. How could Chase trace my credit card and my bank?"

"You asked how I died. He came for me as soon as he escaped, and—" He closed his eyes, masked his face with his hands, and said in a low voice, very quickly, "—tortured me to find out where you were, and killed me."

D.J. hesitated. She looked away. "You knew where I was?"

He sighed. He looked at her. "I shouldn't have, but I wanted to keep track of you. Followed the transfer of ownership on your car through the DMV. I knew your new name and your P.O. box number, the town." He paused, grabbed breath, looked away from her. "He—Doro—he—I didn't want to tell." He pressed his mouth shut, then looked up at her from under his brows. "I couldn't stop myself from saying it. I couldn't stop myself." He closed his eyes tight and thunked fists on his head.

She let go of herself and gripped his fists. Tears spilled down her face. "I'm sorry," she whispered.

"Yes, well, there's no going back, and time is running past us. Pack what you need and let's get out of here."

"Okay." She got her big duffel out of the closet and began throwing clothes into it.

"Can I help?" asked Morgan, the Gary look in his face gone, his voice scared.

"Sure," she said. She looked around, then grabbed one of her spare purses, a big one made of turquoise rip-stop nylon. "Why don't you go in the bathroom and put the stuff from the medicine cabinet in here? Thanks, Morgan. Thanks for everything."

"Some date," he said, but he didn't sound unhappy.

She smiled, then frowned as he disappeared. "Can you ask Gary if I should call the police about this?" she yelled.

"Wait until you find a safe place to call from," Clift called back.

D.J. did a swift job of packing all her favorite clothes and tucking important papers in her purse.

"Here," said Morgan, coming out of the bathroom with a bulging purse. Without pausing for breath, Gary's voice came out: "He's probably watching the building right now, and for sure he'll follow your car, especially if he sees you carrying luggage. I bet he's out there waiting to find out how you've reacted to the note. What does he know so far? No police have showed up, not much of an outcry. Maybe he thinks you're too spooked to do anything about it. Maybe he's coming in to get you right now."

"He doesn't know about you, though."

"We can't know that for sure. I mean, he can't know about

me, Gary, but he might know about Morgan; he knows where you work. Can we stash your stuff away from the apartment? That way someone could pick it up later without tipping him by going into your apartment."

"I have storage space in the basement."

"After that we can drive to a public place and catch other transportation," Gary said. "We should be able to evade him long enough to get you some protection."

With Morgan acting as scout, D.J. carried her things down to the basement, which had an in-building access stairway, and put them in her storage space, pondering whether to pad-lock them in or not. She had never had anything disturbed in the basement. On the other hand, if Chase were here—he had made a science out of sneaking into places where people lived and studying them, while people were present and asleep. Wanting to study people's lifestyles was one curiosity he hadn't bothered to hide from D.J. when their relationship was most intense. His favorite movie was Alfred Hitchcock's *Rear Window*. "Just the little bits of life he sees, don't you love it? All those stories lying there unveiled. You can learn so much by walking around at night and looking in through win-dows."

She stared at her storage space and shuddered. Nothing could keep him from pawing through the skins of her new life. She closed the door and fastened the padlock.

Like a padlock would stop him, any more than her locked apartment door had.

"So where should we go?" she asked, turning toward Morgan, who was standing a few feet away.

At the top of the basement stairs, a man stood backlit by daylight.

3

D.J. gripped Morgan's arm and drew him quietly back toward her. Though there was a light on in the basement, it was dim compared with the daylight coming in through the building's back door. There was a chance Chase hadn't seen that Morgan was down here.

"Yes," said that thrilling rich voice, Chase's voice, that once had fueled her fantasies and later haunted her nightmares, "where should we go?"

D.J. looked around for anything that would serve as a weapon. There was some community property scattered around the common area between the storage closets, things nobody really wanted but had neglected to throw out. She found a dead-headed mop and gripped it with both hands.

His voice sank to a near whisper, curling its way down the stairs. "If you had a choice, where would you go? I want you on my altar, Dorothy Jean. I need you to be my sacrament this time. Only you can give me last rites."

"Young man!" Afra's voice came from somewhere beyond Chase. "Do you have legitimate business in my building? If not, I'll have to ask you to leave."

The shadowed head looked up, away; and then he was gone, his footsteps pounding down the hallway toward the back door of the building.

Finally D.J. let the trembling take her, now that the immediate danger was gone. Her shoulders shook, but her hands were locked around the mop-stick. Breathing fast, she glanced at Morgan, saw that he had moved into the shadow of one of the storage cabinets and was holding a splintery base-ball bat over his shoulder. Something about his expression told her Gary was the one behind the eyes.

"D.J.? You down there? What was that all about? Some young hooligan making an obscene phone call in person?"

At last D.J. drew in a deep breath and lowered the mop. "Afra. Afra. Oh, Afra," she said, her voice quavering. She walked toward the steps and looked up. "Thanks, Afra."

"For what? I did wonder if it was exactly an appropriate moment to bring out my hand-gun, but the way things are these days, I thought it better to be safe."

"Much better," D.J. said, climbing the stairs. Morgan followed her. They both held onto their makeshift weapons. "I have to tell you about him." She glanced down the hall toward the back door, which was still open. She and Morgan ran to look out, heard a car engine growling around a corner, gone beyond sight.

"Sounds like a Beetle," said Saul.

"You know cars?" D.J. asked.

"Any amateur can tell a Beetle," Saul said, "but as a matter of fact, yes, I know cars. One of the few things that kept my interest before I jumped off that bridge in Jersey."

"What's all the fuss about? Who's your young man, D.J.?" Afra said. She was, indeed, holding a large revolver, barrel pointed floorward. "I never heard *him* come in. And I was keeping an ear out."

"Afra, this is Morgan, a friend from work. Morgan, this is Afra, my landlady. Can we go to your apartment? I've got to tell you about that man."

"You vouch for this rude young man?"

D.J. glanced at Morgan. "Oh, yes, Afra. He has rough edges, but he's really very sweet."

Morgan's eyes widened. She knew it was Morgan inside,

158

and that relieved her. She didn't want Saul talking to Afra.

"All right," said Afra. She still looked suspicious. "Come on in."

They followed her into her apartment. Inside, every flat surface that wasn't designed for people to sit or walk on bore treasures from the sea: twisted driftwood, sand-scoured glass, a crab carapace, bowls of water with shining rocks lining the bottom, fragments of sand dollars and shells, gull feathers. The air smelled salty.

"Have a seat. I'll bring you some tea," said Afra, disappearing into the kitchen.

D.J. sat on the couch and tried to figure out how to frame an explanation.

Morgan flopped down beside her, turned on his side so he could watch her. "Miss Deej?" he said.

"Morgan," she said. She smiled at him.

"You really think I'm sweet?"

"You are sweet."

"Not just because of Clift and Gary and Mishka and Shadow and Elaine and Saul and Timmy and Valerie?"

Elaine? Valerie? thought D.J., but aloud, she said, "Just because of you."

"Wow," he said. "Nobody ever said anything like that about me. No girl ever said anything nice about me before."

"Really? Not even the ones inside you?"

"Well," he said, and frowned. "But that's different. It's not like they have a choice."

"Oh, Sweetie," said a new voice from Morgan that D.J. hadn't heard before, a rich husky female voice, "we've got a choice, all right. We could be insulting you all the time; but Deej is right. You *are* sweet."

"Wow," said Morgan. He lay back and stared at the ceiling.

"Who were you talking to?" Afra asked, coming in with a tea tray, a Japanese tea pot and three small handle-less cups.

"Morgan does impressions," D.J. said.

"Really? Who was that supposed to be? Lauren Bacall?"

"They're not famous people," Morgan said, "just people I know."

"Odd," said Afra. "How could you take an act like that on the road?"

"Dr. Dara says it's more like they're different parts of me, or, like, I choose a different voice to express different things."

"D.J. Bubbe," said Afra. "A friend from work?"

"That's not important right now," D.J. said. "What's important is that I have to leave the building, because that guy you chased off knows I live here. He's looking for me. He wants to kill me. He's already killed four other people, Afra. You've been trying to find out about my past, well, here it is. His name's Chase Kennedy. Do you remember the case? He was my boyfriend in my other life, and while he was romancing me, he was murdering other women. I worked with the police to catch and convict him. He was on Death Row last I heard, but today I got messages from him at work, and when I came home, I found a message from him there, and Morgan was just helping me move out when he showed up and you got rid of him. I've got to find someplace to hide."

"Are you serious?" Afra asked.

D.J. stared at her.

Afra said, "He scared off awfully easy."

"He likes being alone with his victims. It's one of his things. Besides, that was a pretty big gun you had."

Afra poured tea. Morgan sat up and accepted a cup. D.J. accepted a cup too, and watched her hostess. After they had sipped in silence for a little while, Afra said, "You're thinking about this wrong. Better if you fort up here, get your protection, keep a vigil; call the police. They could watch outside, catch him trying to get in. There you are. No running and hiding. A running target's a lot more vulnerable than somebody who chooses her own ground."

D.J. looked at Morgan, wondering if Gary had two cents he'd like to toss in at this point.

"If you'll sit there with that gun in your lap, I'll watch out the front window while Doro calls the police," said Gary. "Good thing it's still light."

Afra's eyebrows lowered at this new voice from Morgan, but she set down her cup and retrieved the gun from a drawer by the front door.

"Phone's over there," said Afra, pointing toward the kitchen.

"Gary, you know anyone up here?" D.J. asked, heading for the phone.

"I don't think so."

Afra said, "How come you introduced this boy as Morgan and now you're calling him Gary?"

"Morgan has a different name for each voice, Afra. I know it sounds weird, but . . ." There was no way D.J. could explain this sensibly. Frowning, she paged through Afra's phone book until she found a non-emergency number for the police and dialed.

A woman answered. D.J. pulled herself together. "Hi. I was wondering if you could help me. I think someone's trying to kill me."

The woman listened while D.J. ran the story past her. The woman said someone would be over to check the handwriting on the wall soon.

D.J. hung up and felt despair. How could anybody take her seriously? "Did that sound convincing?" she asked Morgan, wondering if Gary was still in the forefront.

He was. "Don't worry. They should check everything, no matter how strange it sounds. Especially in a community like this one, where there probably isn't a lot going on. You won't have to talk them into it. The evidence will."

D.J. replaced the phone book on the lower shelf of the phone stand. "I sure hope so." She tried to compare herself with people she had observed when they came to be evaluated by Dr. Bollings. No, she wasn't hysterical or tangential; her orientation as to time and place were good; she didn't sound irrational. Of course, some of the most coherent-sounding people turned out to be the really disturbed ones. Maybe her affect was *too* flat. Maybe she should have talked faster.

But really, the situation was absurd.

She remembered the stab of terror she had felt when Chase's voice came from the shadow at the top of the stairs, and she sank down slowly and smoothly until she was sprawled on Afra's rug. *He* was here. He was coming for her. He had killed before. Even Gary hadn't been able to stop him. Nobody knew where he was.

She lay immobilized for a while, her gaze fixed on a water stain on the ceiling that looked like a skull. Her hands and feet felt as if they were miles away, and she couldn't seem to move them.

Sounds came through the cotton over her ears, but for a time she didn't sort them out. A hand touched her shoulder and she jerked, then lay still. A head interrupted her focus on the ceiling. Young face, Fu Manchu mustache, wide worried blue eyes. "Deej? Miss Deej?" the mouth said.

She blinked and noticed that she was breathing.

Afra's face appeared beside Morgan's. "Child? Child, are you all right?"

D.J. brought a hand up, rubbed it over her face. "What happened?" she said.

162

"You kind of fainted," said Morgan, his brows pinched together above the bridge of his nose. "I never seen a girl do that before."

D.J. closed her eyes and tried to reconcile this with her own image of herself. It was hard. "Sorry," she said.

"Good Lord," said Afra, "if anyone ever had an excuse to faint, you do."

"I thought people only fainted because of bad corsets," D.J. said, and tried to sit up. Morgan put a hand under her elbow and helped her. "Thanks," she said, looking at him. Saul's sneer lifted the corner of his mouth, but his eyes looked kind.

A knock sounded on the door, and Afra went over to let a uniformed policeman in. With Saul's help, D.J. struggled to her feet. She looked at him and smiled. He smirked back and pinched her rear.

"You're such a schmuck," she whispered.

"So they say," he whispered back, and slid an arm around her waist. "Put your arm around my shoulders and I'll help you over to the couch."

Furious, she obeyed him. As he let her down on the couch, his hand strayed up to feel her breast so quickly no one could have noticed it except the two of them. "Stop it," she whispered through clenched teeth as he sat down beside her, still smirking. "Think what you're teaching Morgan."

"Exactly," he whispered. "Kid's way too passive."

Afra brought the policeman over. "This is Officer Vance," she said. "Can you talk to him, D.J.?"

D.J. rubbed her eyes, licked her lips. "I guess," she said. When she lowered her hands to her lap, Morgan took one and squeezed it just a little. Glancing at his profile, she couldn't tell who he was. His grip was warm and firm, so probably not Morgan. Even if it was that asshole Saul, she decided, it felt better to have someone hold her hand than to be alone with this. She suspected that Saul was supportive under his abrasive behavior.

Of course, she'd been wrong about a man before.

Still, she held onto his hand and looked at the officer.

Officer Vance was young and sandy-haired, and had a sad long face that made him look as if he belonged in a British comedy: wide blue eyes, long nose, long chin. He took out a notebook.

She told him about the messages at the office, the letter Dr. Bollings had received, the spray-paint upstairs. "I'll never forget his handwriting. And then we saw him."

"What?" His wide eyes went wider.

"He was here in the building. He cornered me and Morgan in the basement, but Afra drove him out with a gun. Then we came in here and called you."

"You didn't tell the dispatcher you'd made visual contact with the subject," said Officer Vance.

"Didn't I? I was having kind of a delayed reaction, I guess."

"She fainted after she hung up the phone," Morgan said.

"Mrs. Griffin, did you see this man?"

"I certainly did," said Afra. "Saw and heard him. Talking trash to D.J. down the stairwell, nasty stuff: like religion, only twisted."

"Can you describe him?"

"A tall fella with a good pair of shoulders on him, at least six feet high, maybe more. He had short dark hair, thick black eyebrows, kind of a narrow face with hollows under the cheekbones. Big hands. He was wearing a green coat that covered up his other clothes, but he had leather shoes, not tennis shoes or whatever they call those things that come in those lurid shades. And he ran away right quick when he saw my gun."

"Your gun?"

Afra got her gun out of the drawer again. The officer made a note.

"Have a sniff," Afra said. "Haven't fired it since my nephew took me target shooting six years ago."

Officer Vance duly sniffed the barrel and handed the gun back to her. "Exactly why did you bring the gun out in the first place?"

"Well, I've got a responsibility to my tenants. I keep track of most things that go on here. I had a very bad feeling about that young fella. He waltzed right in here without so much as a by-your-leave, climbed the stairs, came clattering back down, headed for the basement just like he knew where it was. I don't know. My alarms just went off."

"Do you pull your gun often?"

"First time since about three years ago. There was a squabble in one of the apartments. A man was whaling on his wife, and she was screaming. I called the police, but they didn't come fast enough to suit me, so I went up there and showed him my gun and told him to git. Which he did. And of course she got right after him; they left together the next week." She looked at the policeman. "It's not like I wave this thing around promiscuously. Just when I need to."

"I see," he said dryly. "All right, I think I'm ready to go look at the apartment."

Morgan stood and tugged D.J. to her feet. "Ready for this?" he whispered. He wore Saul's sneer again.

She felt angry. She wasn't sure Morgan could control his ghosts, but she thought, from what Clift had said earlier, that Morgan had some say in who was acting. Why was he siccing Saul on her? Clift, Gary, Morgan, any of the rest of them would have been better, even Mishka or Shadow.

Saul's smile widened. "Yeah, give it to me, baby," he whispered, his hand squeezing hers with steady on-and-off pressure, thumb pressing into her palm, a stand-in for sex, his leer told her.

"Not now!" she muttered, jerking her hand out of his and stalking around the table to the door. She led the officer and Afra and Morgan upstairs, then fumbled for her key, realized she had left her purse in the basement, had dropped it when she grabbed the mop. "Damn," she said.

Morgan reached past her and tried the doorknob. It turned and the door opened.

"Okay. From now on, don't touch anything else, all right?" said Officer Vance.

Maybe there had been a perfect print on the doorknob, D.J. thought. Damn. She led Vance in and pointed to the red spray paint. The message was still there. For a moment she had been afraid that it had disappeared and Vance would think the whole thing was some kind of moronic stunt. But it was still there: "Only you can purify me. Only through your blood will I be saved." Chase's sprawling bold "O's" and "I" pegged the phrases down.

"What does it mean to you, Ms. Hand?" Vance asked.

"I—" Chase had a magic chant that came out of him when the lovemaking was at its most intense. D.J. had never had a traditional religious upbringing, so she wasn't sure exactly what the chant meant. When he said it she was usually pretty far gone into her own sensations, but now she remembered it: "You are my redemption, you are my savior, you renew me and cleanse me, through you I find the kingdom of heaven and I am born AGAIN, oh, oh, wash my sins away."

Later she had thought about it even though she didn't want to. It reminded her of movies about the Catholic Church: confession, then penance and—absolution, was it? Chase had never confessed to anyone; but maybe he knew he'd done something wrong. Maybe he thought of D.J. as a cure for his badness.

It had taken her more than a year to get over the nauseated feeling she got every time someone expressed even the slightest sexual interest in her.

"I think it means he wants to kill me," D.J. said in a thin voice. "He never used to think about me as the—the sacrifice, but I betrayed him. I helped them put him away."

Saul slipped his arm around her and pulled her up against him. She glared at him, her best melt-butter-at-five-paces sizzler, and he grinned and winked at her.

Dimly she realized that she was never nauseated by Saul or even scared of him. Only furious. She dug her elbow into his side, and he relaxed his grip but didn't let go of her. "I helped them put him away," she said in a stronger voice, anger underlying it. "And he should have stayed there. How did he get out?"

"I can't go into detail," said Vance. "But he did escape. He's considered armed and extremely dangerous. Since he's found you here, it might be best if we took you into protective custody."

"Yes," said Morgan, in Gary's voice.

"I'm packed and ready," said D.J. She frowned. "Does this mean I can't go to work?"

"He knows where you work."

"Oh, yeah. Damn! I'll have to call my boss."

Officer Vance said, "Is there anything else you can tell me about his habits that might lead us to him?"

"He drives a Volkswagen Bug," said Saul. "We heard it leaving after Afra chased him off."

Vance's eyes narrowed. He studied Morgan for a moment, then shrugged. "Thanks." He turned to D.J. "Let's get your things."

"They're in the basement."

167

They left the apartment and headed downstairs again, Vance leading the way, followed by Afra, Morgan and D.J. in the rear.

D.J. caught Morgan's arm and slowed him, letting the others get ahead of them. "How come you guys have been letting Saul maul me?" she whispered.

"He makes you mad, and that's better than scared," muttered Clift.

"Prick!" she whispered.

For a second, Clift looked wounded, but then Saul came back, with his nasty grin. "Hey, baby," he murmured, "I know this body ain't much to look at, but I got techniques that could keep you happy."

She felt heat in her cheeks.

"You look great in red," he whispered and laid his hand on her blush.

For a hot furious second she glared at him without moving away. Then something inside her crumbled and she stepped closer, putting her arms around him, pressing her face into his chest. He was crazy. He was haunted. He was probably very bad for her. Maybe she was really bad for him. Morgan was confused enough as it was without some kind of love life.

And yet. In the midst of this crashing chaos, with whatever fragile recovery she'd made since leaving Chase threatening to tear apart, here was wavery Morgan, standing as stable as he could. Even Saul was comforting, in a perverse way. And almost exciting. Which made her want to turn in her enlightened woman's card and hide her face from anybody with self-respect.

"Hon," murmured a woman's voice, tinted with a slight Southern accent and higher than the female voice D.J. had heard from Morgan before, "we can do this later. Maybe we should try not to be too weird right now."

She let go of him and rubbed her eyes. "I—I feel mixed up."

"No wonder. I'm a bit of a blender myself, hon; can't imagine how I'd feel meeting somebody like us, but having that piled on top of this other—" Morgan pursed his lips and looked down toward the front hall, where Afra and Vance stood looking up. "Come on. Sort it out later."

D.J. took his hand and headed down the stairs.

4

"They're monitoring everything. They said this call's okay, since I'm still at the police station. Officer Vance says if you can bring a Dictaphone and the tapes and a computer to the station, they can get them to me. I don't know. You might just want to hire a temp." D.J. paused for breath.

Dr. Bollings said, "I think that would probably be best. How are you holding up?"

"Not too well," said D.J. She stared down at her lap. She was still wearing her office clothes, turquoise and silver shirt, black skirt, dark stockings, black flats. Usually the first thing she did when she got home from work was change into jeans and a big loose shirt. "And—Doc, I did something really stupid." She hesitated.

"Yes?" said Dr. Bollings.

"I made a date with one of Dr. Kabukin's patients. He said he checked it with her, but he told me later that was a lie."

"Oh, Dorothy Jean!"

"I realize it was stupid and probably a violation of office policy."

"Absolutely. But I don't know if we've ever articulated that policy. Tacit understanding isn't the same as something written down." Silence. "Which patient?"

D.J. squeezed her eyes shut. "Morgan," she said in a small voice. Of all Dara Kabukin's patients, Morgan was probably the most obviously askew.

A sigh.

D.J. looked up. Around her the business of the police station went on: people working at desks, some bringing people in, others answering phones, leaving, talking with each other. No one was paying any attention to her. She stared at her skirt, at the black pleats. "Doc, I may be setting Morgan's progress back hundreds of years."

"I'll let Dara know," Dr. Bollings said in a dry voice.

"The more I know him, the more I like him," D.J. said.

"For now, I think your seeing Morgan is contraindicated, at least until Dara has had a chance to meet with him and assess the effects of these developments."

"I don't think I get to see anybody anyway," said D.J. "I'll try to call you again in a couple of days, if it's okay with the police."

"Is there anything else I can do for you?" Dr. Bollings asked.

"Just—" D.J. picked at the pleats in her skirt, staring down, trying to think. She couldn't think of anyone she wanted contacted, certainly not her mother; Afra knew, Gary knew; her other friends, people she had met at community choir, she didn't even know most of their last names or phone numbers. She would have to call the director and tell her she couldn't make it to rehearsal. "Tell Dr. Dara and Dr. Earl and Dr. Brad I won't be in?"

170

"Surely," said Dr. Bollings.

The next day crawled by. D.J. and a female detective named Rae stayed in a cheap hotel, where the odor of cigarette smoke clung to the orange drapes and bedspreads despite wide open windows, and all the light bulbs were forty watts.

"I hate waiting," D.J. said midway through the afternoon after numberless games of cards and Saturday morning cartoons. "Giving all my power over to him. Reacting instead of acting. Are people out there looking for him?"

"You better believe it," said Rae. "Us and the Feds."

"Have they found anything yet?"

"Nothing substantial. We're circulating pictures, asking questions, following leads."

Somewhat comforted, D.J. poured herself some coffee from the thermos on the dresser and sat down to play more cards.

Too restless to sleep long, D.J. was watching the six-thirty a.m. news Sunday morning with the sound down low when she heard about the attack on Afra. In a second she was shaking Rae awake, then turning up the sound. ". . . stabbed seven times. Mrs. Griffin was hospitalized following the midnight assault and is reported in critical condition," the newswoman's voice was saying, while the television showed a picture of the Coat of Arms Apartments building, without identifying its location. "The reason for the attack remains a mystery, but local authorities are warning residents to lock and deadbolt their doors and to be extra cautious about strangers."

D.J. felt frozen. "Why didn't you take the gun to bed with you?" she whispered. "Why wasn't somebody guarding you?

171

Why didn't you come with me?"

Rae was on the phone, talking in a low voice, still rubbing the sleep out of her eyes. D.J. twisted one hand inside the other. She wished Gary were there, talking sense to her, the way he had during the other bad time, telling her she hadn't done anything to make Chase the way he was, that there was nothing she could have done to stop him even if she had known what he was doing, that she wasn't a horrible person just because a monster had chosen her to love. She closed her eyes and clutched her nightgown in her hands and tugged. The fabric was too strong to rip. Why hadn't she figured that he would go after Afra? Wasn't Afra the one who had foiled his last attempt at a kill? Didn't it make logical sense?

Would he go after Dr. Bollings next?

"I have to call," said D.J., surging up off her bed and going to Rae. "I have to call my boss. Maybe he's already gone after her. What about Dara? What about Morgan? I don't think he knew Morgan was there. What if he drove a little distance away and saw all of us coming out of the building? I don't even know Morgan's phone number! But Chase knows everything, he's been watching; maybe he can find Morgan. I don't know where Morgan lives. He killed Gary and Gary was a cop. Gary couldn't stop him. He tortured Gary. He might torture Morgan. Then Gary would have to go through that twice, and everybody else in Morgan, and Morgan—"

Rae shook her shoulders. "Get a grip, D.J."

D.J. blinked and said, "I have to call Dr. Bollings."

"They've dispatched somebody to the residences of all the doctors in the office. They're all fine. We've advised Dr. Bollings and Dr. Kabukin to either leave town or come in for protection—"

"And Morgan?" How could she have gone with the police on Friday night and left Morgan to fend for himself? Even though it had been Gary who said good night to her. "Good," he had said, "now that I know you're safe, maybe I can figure something out."

"Protect yourself," she had told him.

"Oh, I will," he said. He had retrieved the baseball bat.

Tears in her eyes, D.J. had kissed Morgan/Gary good-bye, the first time she'd ever kissed Gary. During the case she had been too emotionally bruised to do anything besides hang onto him, and afterward she had left. Now his desperation matched hers. It had been hard to let go of him.

Yes, if Chase had only driven a little ways away, and had turned back to see that embrace, he would be gunning for Morgan too.

"What if he's already killed Morgan!" she cried, pulling on her hair.

"Shh," said Rae. "Round him up, okay, Rifkin?" She listened, then looked at D.J. "You have an address for him?"

"No. Dr. Kabukin knows, but I don't. Yesterday was our first date."

"Boy," said Rae. "Some fun." She told the person on the other end to check with Dr. Kabukin to get a twenty on Morgan Hesch, and hung up.

D.J. twisted her nightgown. "Is Afra still alive?"

"Not dead, but still critical. Still comatose. One of the other tenants heard a shot and came down and interrupted the attack."

"A shot? Did they find the bullet?" *I hope she killed him!* D.J. thought.

"Yeah. Lodged in a wall. It may have nicked him; the lab results aren't in on all the blood yet."

"He didn't leave a trail, huh?"

"If he did, the paramedics messed it up getting in and getting her out of there."

"Oh, God." Still clutching at her nightgown, D.J. sat on her unmade bed.

A loud knock at the door made her jump, her heart pumping.

Rae picked up her gun and went to the door. Standing to one side, she said, "Who's there?"

"Mitchell," said a woman's voice.

Rae opened the door and let in a short, older woman. "My relief," she said to D.J. "D.J., this is Detective Mitchell."

"You're leaving?" D.J. said, then hated herself for sounding so despairing.

"It's my day with the kid, and I have two weeks' worth of laundry to do," Rae said. "Don't worry. Livvy will take care of you."

D.J. stood up. Business mode, she thought, and held out her hand. "I'm sure she will. Nice to meet you, Detective."

Mitchell had a firm handshake and a no-nonsense face.

Rae dressed. "Downtown'll keep you posted on Mrs. Griffin's progress." Rae picked up a paper sack of her things, shook hands with D.J., and ducked out the door.

Sunday after Rae left was pure hell. By six p.m. D.J. wanted to strangle Mitchell, who was close-mouthed and mean and seemed to resent looking after D.J.

D.J. said, "Come on. You can at least tell me if Morgan's alive or dead."

After fifteen minutes of silence, Mitchell sighed. "They picked him up. He's all right. They've got him in protective custody down at the jail."

"Couldn't he come here?"

"Jail's for his own protection. He's crazy as a bedbug."

Crazy? D.J. felt blank. Then she remembered how Timmy liked to sneak up behind the divider at the office, then leap up

174

with a loud boo and revel in her screams. How sometimes Mishka just sat and sobbed, not even knowing what to do with the tissues D.J. offered her. How Shadow, sounding like an old radio show, was prone to making dark and esoteric pronouncements that didn't make sense once you dissected them. How even Clift could get on her nerves if he watched her too closely and commented on her every move, analyzing the way she bit a pencil or scratched her nose.

That had been before she started talking to him, though. Once they began having conversations, her belief in his craziness had evaporated.

She sighed. She guessed she should just be happy that he was safe, and that the police and the FBI were taking this seriously. After another block of television-filled, conversation-empty time, D.J. said, "Could I go to jail?"

"There's no television in the cells, the beds aren't comfortable, and the food's much worse, but hey, if that's your pleasure, I can take you in."

"I'll pack."

5

Morgan had stubble. He looked pale, sad, and confused. The door to his cell was locked.

"Oh, Morgan!" D.J. said. She turned on Mitchell. "How come he's locked up? He's not a suspect! Is he?"

"No. Like I told you before, it's for his own protection. If you heard the way he was talking . . ."

"Doro, what are you doing here?" Gary said. "I thought they had you farmed out someplace."

"Yeah, they did, but I'd rather be with you. I was going nuts wondering if you were all right."

" 'Course I'm all right. I don't think it's a good idea, your being here. Chase is canny. He could get in here somehow and get you."

"Oh, yeah, Loon? Just how?" asked Mitchell.

"Pose as an informant, a delivery boy, even an officer; get pulled in for something simple like disturbing the peace; if he dyed his hair, accessorized with a mustache, eyebrows, teeth, changed his clothes, he could slip right past you people. You've got other things on your minds."

Mitchell's jaw dropped for a brief second before she closed her mouth. D.J. felt delighted.

D.J. said, "I'm not good at sitting around a room with nothing to do and no one to talk to. Officer Mitchell was with me as a guard, but she's not very friendly. I thought you'd be much more entertaining."

"Undoubtedly," said Clift.

"I could come with you to wherever it was you were," Gary said.

"Officer Mitchell doesn't think so. She says she couldn't keep you under control. How come you convinced everybody here you were crazy?"

"Morgan doesn't coordinate well when he's wakened from a sound sleep," said one of the women, the one with the Southern accent. "I had to do the initial talking, and for some reason that spooked them." Morgan's face smiled. It was another new expression, self-contained and narrow. It reminded D.J. of a cat.

"Are you Valerie or Elaine?" D.J. asked.

"Valerie, sugar."

"Hi."

"Hi, honey."

"Glad to meet you," D.J. said, and Morgan got up and came to the bars, staring into her eyes. His own had a touch of green in them now. She studied them so she would know Valerie again by something other than her voice. She held out her hand. Morgan's lashes fluttered down, then opened again as he took her hand. The little cat smile widened into something friendly.

"Pleased to make your acquaintance, hon," said Valerie. She kissed D.J.'s hand, then looked confused.

D.J. squeezed Morgan's hand. She thought about her talk with Dr. Bollings. "Morgan, what if I'm bad for you?"

"Deej, you're not the problem," said Clift.

"What if I'm making you sicker?"

"Oh, please!" said Saul. "You know we're not sick! In fact, I think you're the only one who knows it besides us. At least I thought you knew it. They brainwashing you, babe?"

D.J. looked away, closed her eyes. It was time to make a decision about this. Dr. Kabukin and Dr. Bollings thought Morgan had some kind of mental illness, and D.J. respected them as professionals. On the other hand, she knew Gary was real, and she felt that all the others had independent existences, too. Time to believe in herself again instead of the experts, after these torturous years of doubting everything she had ever known. She opened her eyes and stared up at Saul. "No," she said, baring her teeth in a nasty grin at him and pinching his cheek. "I know you're not crazy."

"What a load of bullshit!" said Mitchell. "I ought to lock you up for being crazy too!"

"Hey, Morgan, you want to go to a hotel with me?" D.J. said.

His eyes lit up. "Miss Deej!" he said, himself at last. "You're teasing."

"No. All you have to do is prove to Officer Mitchell that

you'll, uh, cooperate, not wander off, obey orders. Not get us in danger."

"There's no way he can prove that to my satisfaction," said Mitchell.

D.J. frowned, wondering if Mitchell had enough power to make decisions about her and Morgan. Business mode, she thought. I put on my persona: I know where everything goes, I am unfailingly polite, organized, relaxed, I can follow the chain of command, I know how to find out what I need to know. I get things done. Business mode. Even though, in her relaxed clothes—Reeboks, jeans, and a big black T-shirt, she wasn't dressed for it. "Who's your superior? Who assigns the duties around here?"

Mitchell snorted. "On a Sunday evening? Good luck."

"Excuse me, Morgan," D.J. said, and wandered out into the main room of the station. "Somebody in charge here?" There were a lot fewer people in the station than there had been Friday night. She headed for the front desk. "Sergeant?"

"Yes?"

"Hi. I'm D. J. Demain. I've got somebody assigned to protect me while this guy, Chase Kennedy, is trying to kill me. Mitchell, the woman who's guarding me, isn't—I just wondered if there was anybody else you could assign?"

He smiled at her and said, "Pleasant isn't in the job description for guarding witnesses, Miss Demain."

"You're right. What I'd really like is for me and my friend Morgan to go underground in a hotel, but Mitchell doesn't think she can handle him. Is self-confidence in the job description?"

"She scared of that skinny guy?" he said.

"Well, he talks in strange voices."

He looked at her for a while, then glanced around the room. "Hey, Harley, you doing anything specific tonight?"

A man in plain clothes who had his feet up on a desk and a *True Romance* in his hands glanced up. "Waiting for anything that might develop," he said. He was a large man with thinning brown hair. He looked sleepy.

"You want to watch a couple of witnesses overnight?"

"They going to do anything interesting?"

The desk sergeant looked at D.J. and raised his eyebrows.

"It's our second date," D.J. said to Harley. "I sometimes go all the way on a second date."

"I'm game," Harley said, lowering his feet and rising. He was taller than D.J. had thought; his clothes were sloppy yet suitable—a biscuit-brown suit, a half-untucked white shirt, a medium-width red tie loosened at the neck. He folded his magazine, tucked it into his inside jacket pocket, and ambled over. "Hello," he said.

"Hello," said D.J., holding out her hand. "D. J. Demain."

"Just call me Harley. I don't tell anybody my first name." His handshake was enveloping but gentle.

"My friend Morgan is locked up. He's the other witness. Could somebody let him out?"

The sergeant handed some keys over to Harley, and D.J. and Harley headed for the jail cells. "You're with the kook?"

"Mmm," said D.J., nodding.

"This does sound entertaining."

Morgan was in a far corner of his cell, curled up nose to knees, and Mitchell was standing close to the bars, glaring at him.

D.J. said, "Hey, Morgan, look what I found! It's Harley. He's taking us to a hotel now."

Morgan scrubbed a hand over his face and unfolded.

"What?" said Mitchell, outraged.

Harley unlocked the door, and Morgan came over, eyes wide.

"Hi, Morgan," said Harley, holding out his hand.

"Hi, Harley." Gary was the one who answered. He grinned and shook hands. "You got any shaving gear? I'm starting to irritate myself."

"We could stop at a twenty-four-hour market on the way over, if you two will crouch down in the back seat while I go in and make the buy."

"No problem," said Gary.

"Either of you have any money?"

"I do," said D.J. She opened her purse and fished out thirty dollars. She handed him the bills.

"Hot damn! We could pick up some doughnuts and hot coffee. Make a shopping list, kids. Let's go."

"Harley, you haven't seen what I've seen," Mitchell said.

"I'm sure that's true," said Harley. "What are you talking about?"

"He's possessed."

"Morgan?" Harley said. "Any truth to the rumor?"

"Yeah," said Gary.

"Demons?"

"No. Ghosts."

"None of them is the Devil?"

"Nope. Just normal people."

"Good. Because that Satanic cult stuff gets on my nerves. If you started chanting in tongues and spewing pea soup I might have to get rough."

"Nothing like that," said Gary.

"Good. Let's go."

Harley made them wait in the stairwell with their luggage while he checked the parking garage. He made them duck down in the back seat before he drove out of the parking garage into the street. "It's likely he saw you come in, D.J.," he said. "Or at least possible. Let's not take any stupid chances."

"Fine with me," said D.J., lying down on the back seat with her head near Morgan's. She was just glad that Harley drove a large American car with lots of leg room.

Morgan peeked at her, and Mishka began giggling.

"Who's that?" Harley said, driving. "That you, D.J.?"

"Uh," said D.J.

"Peek-a-boo," Mishka said at the same time, her voice high and sweet and bubbly. "Peek!"

Harley glanced back over the seat. Mishka hid her eyes with her hands, then pulled her hands aside and said, "Peek!"

"Eerie," said Harley.

D.J. sighed. "That's Mishka. She's three."

"A three-year-old ghost?"

"Eyoo," said D.J., who hadn't considered it like that.

"How'd she die?" Harley said.

"Morgan?" D.J. said.

Mishka's eyes clouded. Her mouth trembled. "Water," she murmured. "Wah wah."

D.J. reached out and stroked her hair. "It's okay. It's okay. Look, now you have a big old body to play in."

Mishka calmed, then disappeared. Saul's sneer showed up in her place. "Don't I, though?" he said, and leered at her.

"Not as big as Harley's," said D.J.

"Low blow, babe."

She smirked at him.

"So who's this one?" Harley asked.

"Saul. Some punk from Jersey." D.J. stuck her tongue out at him.

"Give it to me, baby," said Saul.

"Shut up." She said it lazily, her previous instant fury with anything Saul said gone.

He shrugged and smiled.

"How many are there?" Harley asked.

D.J. tried to count in her head. "Eight?" she asked Morgan.

"Think so," he said in his own voice. "Plus me."

"So who's that?"

"That's really Morgan," D.J. said.

"Whom did I meet in jail?"

"Listen carefully, Buford," said Gary. "Take a wild guess."

The car jerked. The wheels squealed. The car continued driving, though; Harley did not turn around. "No," he said in a low voice.

"Sorry to bring it up this way, Harley. Guess I should have waited till we got to the hotel."

"No," said Harley.

"All right. I'll shut up now. If you want, I don't have to talk to you anymore. Just make sure they get the bastard for me, before he gets Doro."

Without another word, Harley pulled into a parking lot. He turned the car off. After a couple minutes' silence, he said, "Stay down, you two. I'm locking you in. Don't you dare show yourselves." He got out of the car and slammed the door shut.

They lay in silence for a while. Outside the car windows, darkness lay, the edge taken off it by the big lighted sign of the supermarket. The car smelled like vinyl. D.J. realized the night was cold, and wished she had taken a jacket out of her duffel, which was safely locked in the trunk. "Morgan?" she whispered at last.

"Yeah?"

"Gary knows Harley?"

Morgan sighed. "I forgot my speech, even though Dr. Dara taught me and taught me. 'I didn't mean anything by it. Have a nice day.' "

"I don't think that would work on Harley, hon."

Morgan sighed again. Then Gary said, "I consulted with him on a case when he was working up in Seattle. Never knew he was down here now; otherwise I'd have said we should get in touch with him. We've never met face to face, but we spent hours on the phone. Just couldn't resist telling him that way, and I guess I should have. It seemed like such a great joke."

They lay in silence. D.J. wondered what she would do if a face appeared at the window staring down at them. What if it were Chase? She hid her face in the crook of her arm.

A key rattled in the lock, the door opened, and Harley tossed a loaded brown paper bag over the seat-back. Morgan caught it before it could land on D.J.'s head. The car engine growled to life and they were traveling again.

Harley drove erratically for a while, turning corners quickly, slowing, starting, pulling over. They even hit the freeway briefly. No one spoke.

Finally they stopped somewhere else. "Stay down," Harley said in a remote voice, leaving them again. When he came back after a little while, he dropped a key with a plastic tag on D.J.'s head. She grabbed it.

"I've gotten us two connecting rooms, just in case you kids want a little privacy for your second date," Harley said.

"Thanks," D.J. said.

"The rooms are around back where the entrances can't be seen from the road." He started the car again. After a short trip, he turned the engine off and said, "The coast is clear, kids. Let's make a break."

When D.J. tried to sit up, she discovered how stiff she was from an hour of crouching. Harley hauled their things out of the trunk and took them into a room. Morgan groaned and sat up, grabbing the grocery bag. "Do you think he hates me?" he asked.

"No," said D.J. "He's just upset."

"I don't want him to hate me. I like him."

"So do I." She peered out the window, saw that they were in a sheltered spot and she couldn't see anybody else around, just some quiet cars pulled up to anonymous doors in the anonymous dark, lit only by orange outdoor lights placed at intervals along the motel's back face.

"Come on," she said, clutching the key to room 156.

They got out and unlocked the door.

D.J. had to smile. One-fifty-six was a double double. So maybe Harley hadn't taken her absolutely seriously when she told him about its being the second date. She and Morgan had a choice.

She went and opened the connecting door, already unlocked on Harley's side. Morgan closed the room's curtains and turned on a few lamps. This motel was a step up from the one D.J. had stayed in with Rae. There was stationery and a Gideon Bible in the desk drawer, and the light bulbs were at least sixty watts.

From the other room came the sound of television. She knocked on the open connecting doorway and entered when Harley nodded to her.

She said, "I was wondering about Afra's condition. My landlady, Afra Griffin. She was attacked last night. Mitchell wouldn't tell me much about her."

Harley grabbed the phone and dialed, spoke quietly while D.J. leaned against the wall and looked at the television: a TV movie about an abusive husband and a passive wife, with children thrown in for plot complications. Morgan wandered in carrying a Saran-wrapped sheet of mixed doughnuts. "Want to take a shower," he said. He put the doughnuts on the table at Harley's elbow and retrieved his suitcase from where

Harley had left it after unpacking the car.

"Harley's finding out about Afra," murmured D.J.

Morgan gave her a look then, his eyes dark and so wide she could see the whites all the way around the irises, his mouth hanging slightly open. A chill iced her spine: it was the first time he had really scared her. Then he blinked and looked at her from under his eyebrows, a Gary look, put an arm around her shoulders, kissed her cheek, and disappeared into their room. She stood looking after him, her hand to her cheek.

"The news is not good," Harley said as he cradled the handset.

She stared at him.

He got to his feet, walked over, and took her hands. "Come on, sit down," he said, leading her to the bed. She sat, and he sat in a chair across from her, still holding her hands. His brown eyes looked tired. "She's gone," he said gently. "Your friend is gone."

Shock stilled everything in her for a long minute. Then all her connections let loose and she collapsed backward onto the bed, her hands pulling out of his. "No," she muttered. "No."

It's all my fault. If I had never moved into her apartment, if I had never gotten to be friends with her, if Chase had just killed me when he came for me instead of Afra stopping him, maybe she'd be alive today.

Surely death and destruction shall follow me all the days of my life, and I will dwell in the house of chaos forever. Amen.

D.J. put her hands up around her neck and squeezed her throat.

Harley gripped her wrists and pulled her hands away. D.J. coughed.

"You didn't do it," Harley said, holding her wrists.

"It happened because of me." Her voice hurt coming out. Hot tears spilled out of her eyes, streaking down the sides of her head. A moment later she was swallowing choked sobs and trying to twist away from him. He released her and got up. She curled tight, burying her face under her forearms, crying. How could this be? Afra, watering the dahlias, whispering to her that the tenants in 2D were probably going to have a baby, and wasn't it a pity, the way they fought? Afra, sniffing at science. Afra offering her Dutch cocoa on a rainy winter night. D.J. remembered a constellation of photographs in driftwood frames, laughing young men and women, babies, children, that had sat among conch shells on Afra's piano: relatives. Sons? Daughters? Grandchildren? All bereft now. And no chance for her, for any of them, to say goodbye.

"It should have been me," she whispered. She didn't have anybody who'd remember her, except a mother who didn't know whether she was alive or dead anyway, and a ghost.

"It shouldn't have been anybody!" Harley yelled. "Get it through your head! It shouldn't happen at all, but it is happening, and you can't control it! The only one who can control it is Kennedy, until we catch him, and don't you think we blame ourselves—don't you think we know it's our fault that he got away in the first place and that he's getting away with this now?" His face was red with rage.

D.J. rubbed her eyes until she saw purple stars, then looked up at him and detached herself from within. He's upset, she thought. Do I need to be upset now? Maybe I should save it for later. She crushed her anguish down and let control filter to the fore. "I'm sorry," she said in a steady voice.

"Yes, well," said Harley, his voice stabilizing too. He wiped his forehead with a handkerchief. "Best I can do is watch you two carefully, stop it from happening here."

"I'm going to bed now," D.J. said in a small voice.

"D.J." He slumped in the chair. "I'm sorry. That outburst. I'm sorry. I didn't think I would—"

"It's all right," she said.

"No," he said, "but it happened. I'm sorry you lost your friend. Is there anything I can do?"

"I don't—" She pushed herself up, managed to get to her feet. "Can't think of anything. I'm really tired."

"Yes. Leave the door open, kiddo. If you need anything in the night, give a yell."

"Okay." She stumbled into the other room. He followed a minute later, carrying her duffel, and put it on the dresser. The sound of the shower still came through the bathroom door. Harley ambled back into the other room without saying anything else, and D.J. dragged over to her duffel, pulling a nightgown and her toiletries purse out but then lying on the bed with them beside her, without the energy to do anything else.

An arm was around her. D.J. opened her eyes. The last she remembered, she had been lying on her back, but now she was curled up, her nightgown still clutched in her hands, the heat of a body at her back, the soap-clean scent of a stranger in her nose, and a strange arm resting around her, its hand flat on her stomach. Light leaked from the bathroom; all the other lights in the room were out. She glanced down at the arm, saw it was a man's, naked, thin but sinewy, with a growth of fine black hairs on it. She lay for a while staring straight ahead at the wallpaper, which had a faint rick-rack pattern, brown on beige. It came to her that Afra was dead. A black knot twisted her stomach, and hot tears seeped from her eyes. She let go of the nightgown and put one hand on

Morgan's hand on her stomach. He murmured something and pressed up against her back, digging his chin into her shoulder. Suddenly she wanted to be held more than anything else. She lifted his hand and rolled over to face him. He had shaved. His eyes were closed, and his slow breath flickered the ends of his mustache.

"Valerie?" she murmured. "Valerie?"

After a moment his eyes opened. It was too dark for her to see their color. "Hon?" murmured Valerie.

"Could you hold me, please?"

Valerie stretched and yawned, patting her mouth as she did. Morgan was wearing a pair of jockey shorts, nothing else. He looked more muscular naked than he ever had inside his clothes. Valerie put her arms around D.J., stroking her back in soothing circles.

D.J. closed her eyes and relaxed, curled against Morgan's front. After a long moment, she said, "Afra's dead."

"I know, sugar. I know." The massage was smooth, calming. D.J. drifted back to sleep.

Daylight was sifting through the curtains. D.J. woke up feeling sticky. Her mouth tasted like moldy cheese. Morgan was asleep. D.J. slid out of his arms, grabbed her purse, and went into the bathroom.

She felt much better after a shower, deodorant, baby powder, and teeth brushing. She was ready to eat something, anything. She wondered if Harley had eaten all dozen doughnuts in the night. After sliding into her sweaty T-shirt, she sneaked back out and ransacked her duffel for other clothes, then retreated to the bathroom again, glancing at Morgan before she shut the door. She stopped when she realized his eyes were open and he was looking at her.

"Pasty," said a new voice coming from his mouth.

"What?" D.J. straightened. She clapped a hand over her mouth, felt her eyes going wide.

Morgan struggled up on his elbows. He squinched his face up, then relaxed it into a frown.

"Too soon," said Clift, rumbling a little. "Way too soon." Evidently he wasn't good at mornings. He waved a limp hand at D.J. "Go get dressed."

D.J. ducked into the bathroom and dressed slowly. The new voice. Familiar.

Afra's.

6

"Morgan?" she said when she came out of the bathroom. She had picked one of her dresses to wear today, a crush-proof comfortable polyester number in burgundy.

Morgan had pulled on jeans and had his head bent forward, brushing his hair down over his face. "What?" asked the Lauren Bacall voice from beneath the hair.

"Elaine?" said D.J., sitting on the bed beside Morgan. The voice wasn't Valerie's; it sounded deeper, devoid of accent, and smokier.

"Mm-hmm," said the Lauren Bacall voice. "I'm the hygiene nut." She tossed her head back and brushed the hair out of her face. "You should have seen this boy before I got here. Talk about socially unacceptable!"

"Does he like it, that you—take care of him?"

" 'Course! He's grateful. He's not stupid, you know; he realizes that this kind of maintenance makes people accept him more. Nobody else ever taught him these things. Mostly his mother just left him in the basement and told him not to make any noise." She finished brushing. "Got a rubber band, sis?"

D.J. searched through the purse Morgan had filled with her bathroom supplies, found the pouch with hair things in it. D.J. wore short permed hair at the moment, but she had had her long hair days, too, until she got tired of having to deal with it all the time. She handed Elaine a braided elastic loop, and Elaine twisted it around Morgan's long black hair, making a ponytail down the back.

"Normally he likes the jungle look, so he can hide behind his hair if the moment demands it. But I think we can do without that today," Elaine said.

Harley stood on the threshold of their room and knocked on the door sill. "Decent?" he said.

Morgan's lip lifted in Saul's sneer, but he didn't say anything out loud.

"Come on in," D.J. said. "I'm starving."

Morgan looked through his suitcase and pulled out a white shirt with billowy sleeves, like the shirts pirates wore in Errol Flynn movies. "Eh?" Saul said, as he held the shirt up to his chest, lifting one of the sleeves, shaking the lace-edged ruffled cuff at her.

"Who does your shopping?" asked D.J.

"It's a constant battle," Saul said. "Mostly we shop in thrift stores, so we can get a piece of clothing for each of us." He slipped the shirt on over his head. "I don't think our style makes us popular at parties. The bits don't go together."

"Does that voice trick work for you or against you?" Harley asked.

"What do you mean?"

"You could put it all together into some kind of act, if you had a writer. It's uncanny how different your voices are."

"That's what I thought," Afra said. "Lots of potential."

D.J.'s face prickled and her fingers tingled.

"Shut up," said Clift. "Not yet." He sat down on the bed next to D.J. "You're pale. We're sorry, Deej. I know it's a shock. It's a shock to us too, every time this happens. We haven't settled in yet."

D.J. gripped a fold of her dress, staring down at the material. "There's some kind of selection process, isn't there? I mean, not every single person who dies comes and gets inside you, only special ones — otherwise you'd be legion, right? You have ghosts from all over the states! How do you pick them?"

"I suspect a prerequisite for it is that we have to believe in ghosts, one way or another, to become them," Clift said. "Another thing that distinguishes us from garden variety ghosts is that we are impregnated with some sense of mission, at least initially. Violent death seems to have quite a bit to do with it. Then there's resonance. Morgan isn't the only ghost magnet in the world, but he emits a certain resonance that appeals to a select few, namely those of us here. In effect, there's quite a strict entrance exam."

She twisted her dress between her hands. "Does Morgan have any say about this?"

"I want her," Morgan said. He patted D.J.'s shoulder. "I like her. She's real nice. You want her to go away, Miss Deej?"

"No, of course not," she said, turning to look at him through a glaze of tears. "I can't quite understand it yet, but I'm glad she's here. But I just worry about you, Morgan. It must be so crowded inside you."

"I have all these friends to talk to," he said.

"But what if they all want to talk at once?"

"I tried to introduce us to Robert's Rules of Order, but the others say that's silly," Clift said. "If we didn't like each other, this would be a nightmare. However, I admire all of us."

"Even Saul?"

"Oh, yes. He's a pain in the butt, but he doesn't mean anything by it. He has certain strengths the rest of us don't."

Harley vanished into his room and returned with half a dozen doughnuts, which he offered to D.J. and Morgan. D.J. grabbed three cake doughnuts. Morgan took one glazed twist.

"Aren't you, like, eating for twelve?" Harley asked Morgan.

"Most of us don't care for sweets," said Clift. "This is for Gary."

"Oh, God," Harley said, sitting down at the table. "Gary." He mopped his forehead with a handkerchief. "I think I better get this straight now. D.J., you buy this whole ghost-possession thing?"

"Yes," mumbled D.J. around a mouthful of doughnut.

"Even though it makes no sense."

"I don't think I can explain it any other way. Besides, Gary—"

"Gary?"

"I knew Gary in San Francisco, Harley. He says he consulted with you on a case while you were in Seattle. Were you in Seattle before you came to Spores Ferry?"

"Oh, God," said Harley.

"How could he know that if he wasn't Gary?"

"Maybe he's psychic."

"You accept psychic but you don't believe in spooks?"

"I don't know what I believe." He stared at Morgan. "Gary?"

"Buford?"

Harley cringed. "Don't call me that!"

"Heh heh heh." Gary wolfed his doughnut. "Okay, Harley."

"You used to be a sensible guy," Harley said after a pause. How the are hell are you surviving this? Surviving. Is that the word? If that *is* you in there, isn't it driving you crazy?"

Gary frowned and stared at the rug. After a long silence, he said, "I woke up." He glanced at Harley. "You know how I died?"

"Heard," said Harley.

Gary looked at D.J., then shrugged. "I never wanted to feel anything again. The sleep was such a relief. I think I stayed in it for a while. Fact, Clift tells me I was gone, nowhere, null, a couple weeks, before I woke up.

"Probably the last thing I was thinking about besides pain was Doro. I knew the boyfriend was looking for her, and I had aimed him right at her. I opened my eyes, and there she was. There you were," he said, looking at D.J., "at least the top of your head, over that wall. Hair color and style changed, but then you looked up, and there were those eyes. Never forget 'em."

She stared at him, a trembling smile surfacing.

"I couldn't figure out how that happened. Which was the dream? Death, or waking up? Then all these people started talking to me, all these strangers, big blonde woman, little baby girl, professor type, black kid, a whole bunch of them, saying, 'Settle down! Settle down, brother, let us explain.' "

He sat still for a while, staring toward the curtains, then frowned and glanced down at his hands. "Well, it was one wild explanation. But you know . . ." He looked up at Harley, smiled. "It's nice in here. Never been close to so many people. I was a loner before, and I thought this was my worst nightmare, but actually—"

Harley shuddered. "More power to you."

Gary burst out laughing, leaned against D.J. She smiled, finding his joy infectious.

"Know what?" Gary said when he had stopped laughing. "I can't even buy a beer."

Harley frowned. "Do you want one?"

"Not especially. It just strikes me as—" He shook his head, smiling. "And voting. Boy. Can't wait to see how we handle that. And registering for Selective Service?" He frowned. "We do that yet?" He listened to something D.J. and Harley couldn't hear. "Oh, of course, we'd qualify for an exemption." He shook his head. "Kid's been in therapy for three years already and he's only nineteen. Nobody gets a normal adolescence."

"Cut to the chase," Clift said.

"Sorry," said Gary. "Right. The point is to stop the boy-friend."

"Already a lot of people working on that."

"We have certain resources they don't have."

"Like what?"

Morgan drew in a deep breath, sat up straight, licked his lips. Afra said, her voice tight with pain, "My name is Afra Griffin. He came to my apartment."

Harley's eyes went wide. He hunched his shoulders.

"His hair was different. Blond. It was the middle of the night, and I was asleep. I had my gun on the bedside table, on a shelf you couldn't see without being in the bed. He didn't know. He taped my mouth. He tied me." She glanced at D.J., stopped. She looked at Harley. "Gary said it was his standard M.O. They probably told you all that. I got a hand free, but by that time he, well, I couldn't aim as well as I used to. Shot him in the arm. Right forearm. Stopped him. He had to go tie a bandage around it, and then noise came from upstairs. Shot woke up the Lutzes. So he scampered out of there."

Her eyes closed, and her face tightened, as if suddenly Morgan were all cheekbone and temple. She opened her eyes. "He asked me things at first. Where D.J. was. He'd rip the tape up off my mouth so I could answer, then put it down again. I told him you went with the police. Then, when I didn't have any more answers, then, he just . . ."

She shook herself. "Here's what I remember. He was wearing gray pants, a white shirt, red suspenders. He had bleached his hair platinum blond since the day before. By the time he left, his shirt was bloody and his pants were too. So he would have had to change them, either dump them or clean them. He had a big army overcoat he took off before he started on me, and he wrapped up in it before he ran away. I heard that Beetle noise, like Saul said. VW Bug. So. You're looking for a blond who drives a VW and wears a full-length army jacket, olive drab. He's got a gunshot wound in his right forearm."

"I'll phone that in."

Gary said, "What are you going to tell them when they ask where you got the information?"

"A witness." Harley struggled to his feet. "Don't worry. I can make this fly somehow. I'll be right back."

D.J. turned to look at Morgan, took his hands.

"You told me he did impressions," Afra said, and smiled.

"That sounds more believable than the reality, doesn't it?"

Afra rolled her eyes, something D.J. had seen her do a dozen times in her previous incarnation. It meant: *what a world, what a world.* She said, "You see, I've been telling them Harley's right. We could put an act together, if we had the right script. Did I ever tell you I used to be in the theater?"

"You never did," said D.J.

"Morgan doesn't know what he wants to do when he

grows up," Afra said. "From what he tells me, he's just sampling various classes in school. I think we have a future in stand-up, but I haven't convinced any of the others."

"A bit too public for my palate, sugar," said Valerie, distaste in her voice. "I would vastly prefer it if we just kept our little oddities to ourselves."

"Yes, but we never do," said Clift.

"That's because of Timmy and Saul," Valerie said. She wrinkled her nose. "I wish those boys would observe a few civil niceties. And you, Cliffie, have the lecture habit."

"I don't think I could give it up if I tried, Val."

"Oh, I don't know," Valerie said in a considering voice. "I just think we haven't found the proper motivation yet."

Harley wandered back in. "Well, they took notes when I talked to them. Seems like they think insanity is contagious, and that I caught it from you, Morgan. Somebody'll be along soon with some real breakfast, D.J."

"Good," she said, her stomach chiming in with a rumble, even though she had tried to quiet it with the doughnuts. "I forgot to get any dinner yesterday."

"McNamara will bring us something good. Wonder what's on TV." He went toward the television and D.J. had a terrible sense of *déjà vu:* watching the news Sunday morning, hearing about the attack on Afra. What if the news this morning brought more evil? Whom had she forgotten to protect this time?

"Don't," she said in a little swallowed voice. And not only that, but right after the television announcement, Rae had disappeared. "Harley!" she cried. "Are you going to leave us too?"

"What?" he said.

"Like Rae. Yesterday. Suddenly someone came along and relieved her. I know you shouldn't have to work twenty-four hour days or anything, but I just . . ."

"Oh, that? No, I told downtown I'd stick with you, at least for the next two days. I may need a little time off now and then. Couple hours to go feed the cat, collect the mail. But I figured nobody else is going to make the adjustment I did."

"Meaning me?" Gary asked.

"Yeah. I still don't quite believe in you, but I do give you credibility. I think other people could easily make a mistake about you."

"They do all the time," Clift said.

Harley nodded, frowning. He looked at the television, now in reach, then glanced at D.J. "You don't want me to turn it on?"

"I don't want to hear that there's been another attack."

"I've already talked to downtown today, and they would have told me. Let's just check in with one of the morning programs. I need a news fix."

"Okay," said D.J. She looked at Morgan. "Any of you play cards?"

"I know one called Misery," said the Shadow's deep echoey voice.

"You'll have to teach me," D.J. said. She had never had an extended conversation with the Shadow. She wondered how he had died, who he had been. He couldn't really be an old radio play character, could he? Getting to know Morgan would take a lot of time and work.

"With great pleasure," the Shadow said.

"So which one's that?" asked Harley, glancing away from Regis and Kathie Lee.

"Shadow," D.J. said, as the Shadow geared up and produced his long spooky laugh that started at a medium pitch and sank down into very low registers.

Harley made a face as if he had smelled something bad.

"Oh, come on," said D.J. "He's just a kid. How old are you, Shadow?"

He glared at her. "Sixteen." It was the first time she had heard him say something in a normal voice. He sounded sullen and young.

"You can sound scary if that's what you want," she said. "How do we play Misery?" She retrieved Rae's cards from her luggage and began shuffling.

"Deal thirteen to each," he said in his spookiest voice.

They were playing their second hand when a knock came on the door of Harley's room. Harley switched off the television, reached for his gun, and eased to the connecting door. "Who's there?"

"Breakfast," said a voice through the door.

Panic started in D.J.'s chest and spread through her like fire feeding on lines of oil. She stared at Morgan. Morgan laid his cards down and looked out from under his brows.

"Don't open the door," D.J. whispered to Harley. Morgan was on his feet, carrying his body with a focus and intensity foreign to him. "It's him."

7

D.J. crept across the bed and picked up the phone. She felt as if she had swallowed a stone, and it lay in her stomach, pinning her down. She could not escape. Why even think of it?

Calm, she was calm. She had Things to Do. She dialed 911. Morgan walked silently to the outside door of their room. He gripped the knob.

"Breakfast?" said Harley in a sleepy voice. "I didn't order

any breakfast. You sure you got the right room?"

"Ambulance, fire, or police?" said a voice in D.J.'s ear.

"Police," she whispered. She realized that she didn't even know what hotel they were in, or the address, having come in blind the night before. She grabbed an ashtray off the bedside table and fished the matchbook out of it. "I'm D. J. Demain, a protected witness, here with Morgan Hesch and Detective Harley." She studied the matchbook. "We're at the Lamplighter Inn, 1342 Benjamin Boulevard: and Chase Kennedy, the escaped murderer, is trying to get into our room. Room 154, around the back. Please send help." She cradled the phone silently.

Morgan was watching Harley for a cue. Chase's voice said, "Room 154, that was my instruction from Detective McNamara." Chase sounded honestly confused. "But I'll leave if you want me to."

D.J. felt cold. Chase knew the detective's name. Had he killed him? How else would he know where to come? If he had done something to the detective, he probably had the police car, the gun, the radio; he had found her job, and her apartment. There was no escape. She closed her eyes and shivered. She remembered this kind of cold from before, the Arctic place she had gone when she realized Chase was who he was and she had made all these wrong assumptions, when she had learned she could never trust herself again. She had lived with this cold for a long time before anger thawed her out. Maybe this brief tropical period had been an illusion.

"Wait a sec," said Harley, his voice still sleepy. "What kind of breakfast you got?"

Morgan whispered, "Doro, get in the bathroom and lock the door."

She stared at him. How could she leave him alone out here with Harley and Chase? How could any of them be here?

What if Chase did something awful, shot Morgan and Harley? There was no escape.

She felt so cold . . .

Maybe she could stop Chase somehow. It had happened before. She had to remember that. Maybe if she wasn't out here Morgan and Harley would both die and Chase would get away. Again. More deaths on her head. No, she couldn't stand that. Not again.

Anger sparked somewhere inside. She could fight. She could go down fighting.

"Do it," Morgan/Gary whispered.

She didn't have any special defense training, and she knew she wasn't as strong as Chase physically. Much as she hated to admit it, she could help Morgan and Harley best by being out of the way and as safe as possible. She scooted into the bathroom and locked the door, then looked through her toiletries purse for weapons. A perfume bottle. She could spritz that in Chase's eyes if he somehow got through the door. Baby powder. Throw it in his face. Cold cream: squirt it on the floor in front of the door and make it slippery? She did it, spreading the pale goop with her hands. She lined up the rest of her arsenal on the counter, then worked the towel bar out of its holders. Whatever else happened, she wanted to take a big swipe at him, break his nose at least, his head at best, his balls.

She sat on the closed toilet, the towel bar over one shoulder, and listened. Anger burned slow and steady.

What happens if I die? Morgan wondered. Gary had the body; they all thought that was best; nobody was going to argue at a time like this. Gary had faced situations like this before. He was tense but relaxed.

If I die, Morgan thought, we all die. He thought about

each of his insiders, all their differences, all their samenesses; how Mishka loved ice cream and Elaine hated it, but put up with it for Mishka's sake; how Timmy taught the rest of them to play hopscotch, which a few could remember from grade school days but most had forgotten; how Valerie loved wind and wanted to run out into the middle of it any time it was blowing; how Afra knew the names of every flower, and the Shadow the names of every comic book hero; how Saul was hot for anything female, but usually wilted if any of them gave him a second look; how Clift liked to confuse people who thought Morgan was stupid by being smarter than they could ever be; how Gary liked to laugh, so deep it felt like it came from his toes.

He couldn't die. He barely even knew Afra and Gary yet. Where would all the insiders go if they lost him?

Gary clenched his jaw, feeling fire sear through his muscles. He wanted to kill Chase, stamp him out, crush him. He wanted to whip welts into him, smash his head between two rocks and destroy that corrupted brain. He drew in long draughts of breath, trying to calm himself, but it was difficult. Hadn't he come back just to do this one thing? What else was there? His goal was just the other side of a door. All he had to do was open the door and grab.

"Maybe, if it's a real good breakfast, I'll open the door," Harley said. "I guess I am kind of hungry."

"Sorry. Just McDonald's, but there's a lot."

"Sounds great," said Harley. "What's the password?"

"Password?"

"Yeah, you know, there's always a password."

"The password is—" The sound of a shot.

"Go!" yelled Harley to Gary, backing into room 156 and

slamming the connecting door shut, locking it. Gary opened the outside door, glanced out, stood back as Harley took a look out. Then Harley, gun in hand, ran past Gary.

Peering around the doorsill into Room 154, gun aimed in, Harley said, "Drop it."

A shot answered him, smashing into his car where it stood parked in front of the door. Harley fired an answering shot and ducked back. Two more wild shots sounded from Room 154, with no provocation. "Lucky he favors knives," Harley muttered to Gary. "No aim. Get me a pillow."

Gary opened and closed his fists, then, blowing out breath, went to get a pillow.

A head poked out of room 152. Harley gestured the man away, hoping he would take the hint and hoof it out of range. He glanced behind him, saw someone else peering out. He flashed his badge and the person ducked out of sight.

Gary handed him a pillow. Harley held it out in front of 154's open door, attracting two more shots.

Harley jerked the pillow back, whispered to Gary, "Sound like a service revolver?"

"Uh-huh."

"Six shots. With the one he used to shoot open the door, that should do it. I think Mac carried a revolver. You think he knows how to reload?"

"He always used knives," Gary said, his voice flat and harsh. He noticed the police cruiser pulled up behind Harley's. The heat inside him was making him light-headed. He was having trouble paying attention, finding it impossible to drop down into the cool, calculating mindset he had used when police work had demanded it before.

"I'm pretty sure I winged him," Harley muttered. He edged close to the door and yelled, "Throw the gun out or I'll open fire."

Sounds of movement, the skitter of a wheel on one of the beds as the furniture shifted.

"Come on," Harley said, "we have you trapped, and you're out of bullets. What are you going to do? Might as well give up."

The revolver clattered out the door to land on the concrete walkway outside.

"Okay. I'll be coming in now," said Harley. "Don't do anything foolish." He peeked around the edge of the door. The sound of a rifle cocking sent him jumping back. The rifle blast smashed the grill of his car.

Two more cruisers pulled up, lights revolving, sirens silent. Car doors opened, cops hiding behind them. "Got him trapped in room 154," Harley yelled, "but he's got a rifle. Stay out of the line of fire."

He turned to Gary. "Get D.J. out of here," he said.

Gary wanted to argue. He flexed his fists, wishing Morgan had more muscle. Gary wanted to get his hands around Chase's neck, watch as the life left his body. How could he trust Harley to get Chase, when Gary couldn't even trust himself? He had known Chase was going to kill him, but he had given Chase the information he wanted anyway. He knew he would have done anything Chase asked in the end, just to get the pain to stop.

He needed to destroy Chase. He never wanted to face that dark weak place in himself again.

"Get her out of here," Harley said again.

Gary closed his eyes. The rage was so hot inside him he couldn't think straight. "Come on," whispered Valerie. "Consider Doro. Life's more important." In the dark stage that was Morgan's mind, Valerie reached out and touched Gary's forehead. Her fingertips were cool. The red rage ran out of his soles as cool flowed from her hand. Gary took a deep breath, nodded to Harley, then went to knock on the bathroom door. "Come on, Doro, we have to run."

"Is it really you?"

"Who else? Come on!"

She opened the door a crack and looked out, towel rod at the ready. He grabbed her wrist and pulled her out the door. They ran away from the room where Chase was trapped and around the side of the building.

"Where are we going?" she demanded, still gripping the towel rod. "What are we doing? All we need is a tank. We could ram right through the building and run over him. Turn him into slime." Her breath was coming in ragged gasps and her face was bright red.

Gary said, "It's almost over. He's trapped. He's got to surrender or he's going to die." His voice was tight with residual rage. He still felt a terrible need to go back, walk into the hail of fire, and take Chase out himself.

"We can't leave now!" D.J. said.

"We can't help, Doro. Somebody else will do it."

"What if they don't? What if he gets away again?" A tear streaked down her face. "What if it starts all over?"

He took a deep breath and let it out, then gathered her into his arms, wishing he had Valerie's healing touch, wishing Doro's arguments didn't echo his own. He could feel how stiff and tight she was, but after a long moment her shoulders eased, relaxed.

"I hope he dies," she whispered. "Can't trust prison to hold him. I don't think I could stand it if this happened again. I'd kill myself first."

"Sometimes that's not a final solution," Saul muttered.

"Shut up," Clift said. "Deej, we have to delegate this time. Lord knows *we're* used to that. We have to trust somebody else to do the job for us."

After a silent moment, she said, "I just want it to be over."

They stood quiet for a little while, and then he sighed and released her. He said, "Let's go to the motel office, get the evacuation of the other rooms in motion."

D.J. sat in the waiting area of the motel office drinking instant Sanka and trying to relax. Every time she let her mind go, she thought of Chase; legions of "what-ifs" rattled their spears, pricking her composure. Instead of thinking, she stared at her hand, watched it shake as it held the coffee cup; watched the tremoring of the dark liquid.

Morgan sat down beside her on the ratty brown couch, staring at the police officer at the motel desk. The officer had a hand-held radio, and he was talking alternately into it and the phone. Tension radiated from him.

D.J. handed Morgan her coffee cup. "Unleaded," she said.

He took a sip, grimaced.

Distant pops sounded. The officer at the desk tensed.

Morgan jerked and dropped the paper cup. Coffee spilled on the brown rug.

"Morgan?" D.J. said.

Morgan stared at her, his eyes so wide she could see the whites around the irises, his mouth open slightly.

D.J. went cold, remembering the last time he'd given her that look. She couldn't look away. He seemed frozen in position, one of his hands clutched tight on the couch's arm, the knuckles white with strain, the other hand biting into the couch cushion between him and D.J.

"Morgan," she whispered.

A voice came from the police radio. The officer listened, his eyes closed in concentration, shoulders hunched. Then he blew out breath and stood up. "It's over."

205

D.J., staring into Morgan's unblinking wild eyes, knew the officer was wrong.

8

Harley staggered into the office and headed straight for the coffee table. He had lost his suit jacket somewhere, and sweat dripped from his forehead, patched his shirt under his arms and suspenders. After he had mixed up a cup of instant from the hot water in the big pot, he turned to D.J. and Morgan.

Morgan was leaning back on the couch, his head lax, only white slits of eyes showing. D.J. sat forward on the edge of the couch, her face chalky, her eyes dark, her hands clenched on one another.

"You don't look relieved," Harley said.

"The fight's here," she whispered, and glanced toward Morgan without turning her head.

"Shee-it!" said Harley. Clift's list of qualifications for ghost-possession came back to him: believe in ghosts; have a mission; violent death; resonate right. "They wouldn't invite him in!" he said.

"He's never waited for an invitation."

Morgan's jaw worked, made a clicking nose. His mouth closed. His eyelids fluttered, then opened, their pale blue stained with brown. "Puny," he said, his voice low and thrilling. He flexed his hands, then looked around. "Dorothy Jean! At last! You don't know what I've gone through to get to you."

"Yes, I do," she said. "Get out! Die, Chase! Just—die!"

"I already did that," he said. His face darkened. "It hurt, and not in a good way."

"Get out of Morgan!" She pulled her hands apart, made fists, and began pummeling Morgan's chest.

"Hey! Is this any way to treat the one who loves you? Although it does feel so good." He smiled at her. Suddenly she remembered one evening, before she knew much about Chase. They were having a candlelight dinner at her apartment. She had made a spectacular meal, because she was sure Chase was the one she'd been looking for all her life, and the way he responded to her had her convinced he felt the same way about her. They had finished dessert and were looking at each other. D.J.'s mind, at least, was in the bedroom, where she had covered the lampshade with a pink scarf and left some sandalwood-scented candles burning.

Chase picked up one of the candles on the dinner table and tilted it so that hot wax poured onto his palm. "Mmm," he said. "So good. So good." He slowly dripped a circle on one palm, then switched hands and dripped more wax on the other. Wondering if it was some erotic turn-on she'd never heard of, D.J. had picked up the other candle and tried dripping a drop on her own palm. At the stinging pain of the burn, her hand jerked. She set the candle upright and looked at Chase with horror; he was so absorbed in what he was doing that he never noticed. She blinked. Maybe she was hypersensitive to pain. Maybe that was it.

Pretending she had to go to the bathroom, she went to her room and blew out the candles there. People did have different ideas of pleasure, she told herself, but she didn't want him practicing his brand on her.

Still, she had thought Chase was near enough to perfect not to worry about.

She stopped pounding on him. He gripped her shoulders,

drew her against him. "The hair, you have to change that," he said. "It's ugly. Not like an angel's anymore. But now you're a dirty one. I forgot. Now you're a dirty one." Then he ground his mouth against hers, forced hers open and thrust his tongue in. After her first startled fury, she was going to bite down on his tongue, but Harley grabbed her from behind and pulled her out of Chase's arms.

"Gary!" Harley said. "Can't you do something?"

Chase laughed. "Invoke your little police friend," he said. "I killed him once, and I'll do it again."

"Clift?" asked D.J.

"Detective?" said a strange voice from behind them. D.J. and Harley turned.

A uniformed officer stood there. "They need you for testing," he said.

"Something's come up," said Harley. He reached behind him, then turned to Morgan and handcuffed him. "I need to question this witness before I wrap it up. I suggest we go somewhere more private," Harley said to D.J. He turned back to the other officer. "Okay if we borrow your cruiser, just to sit in?"

The man shrugged, then held out keys. "Right there," he said, pointing a thumb over his shoulder.

"Thanks, Fletcher. This shouldn't take long." He dragged Morgan up off the couch by the handcuffs, then took him outside and pushed him into the back seat. "Sit up front, D.J.," he said, climbing into the car.

She got in beside him and looked back through the divider at Morgan. "Can't you do something?" she asked, not knowing to whom she was appealing.

"I'm trying, Deej!" cried Clift. He gulped.

"The little professor," Chase said. "I'll step on him like a bug. The sluts I shall slit from crotch to throat. I missed my chance to do that to the old lady, but now that I have another chance, I'll do it correctly. I haven't decided what to do to that pesky nine-year-old boy yet, but it's delicious to think about my options. And the baby. I don't know if she's dirty yet." He frowned. "But she will be. Maybe not right away. But after I deal with the others." He sat back and smiled. "The cop. The cop. He was so much fun the last time. I'll make it even better this time."

"Morgan!" D.J. said. "Kick him out. Kick him out."

Morgan blinked, then looked at her with his own pale blue eyes. "Kick him out?" he said in a slow voice.

"You don't want to keep him, do you?"

"No! I don't like him at all."

"Kick him out."

"I don't know how."

"Ask the others."

"Okay." Morgan closed his eyes.

D.J. sat back. Business mode, she thought. Business mode. Everything has a place; how do I get rid of something that doesn't belong? Delete it on the computer. Shred the file. For a minute she visualized Chase as a paper ghost, going into the shredder whole and coming out as narrow crimped strips of paper. See him get out of that one.

Dump the trash. Edit the bad phrases out of the report. But Morgan wasn't a computer.

What would Dr. Kabukin do?

What was she always trying to get Morgan to do? Integrate. And Clift said no; it would make them all disappear, and leave Morgan confused. What if they each grabbed a piece of Chase and wouldn't let go, though? Maybe if they pulled him to pieces, the pieces would be easier to get rid of.

Shredding.

"Morgan," said D.J.

"I'm trying to kick him out but he won't go! Even Gary can't hold him!"

"Morgan, integrate him."

"What?" He sounded panic-stricken. "I don't want him in here!"

"Each of you take a different piece."

"No! I don't want anything he has!"

"Is what you're doing working?"

"No! We keep trying to beat him up, but he's stronger. He's awful, D.J. He looks around and everything he sees is ugly and he makes us look at it like that and we can't find our own eyes. He looks at us and we're all ugly. And we get all weak when he looks at us like that! All my insiders had ugly places in their vision, but we talked about them and they got better, but he won't let us talk, he won't listen, he just hurts us and hurts us—"

"I know."

"He's going to poison us!"

"Yes. But maybe if you all integrate him, the doses will be small enough for you to survive. Clift said integration would destroy your insiders."

"Destroy . . ." Morgan closed his eyes again.

After a long moment of restless silence, Morgan opened his mouth. "Dorothy Jean!" cried Chase. "Never forget. I always loved you, even after you betrayed me. I love you now even though you've betrayed me again. My lamb, my savior, my Judas—"

"Shut up!" said D.J., fighting tears and anger.

Morgan began coughing and choking. Harley climbed out of the car and opened the back door, standing back a respectful distance, but watching Morgan.

What have I done? D.J. thought. If they take the pleasure he had killing those women, if they take that he likes pain, if they find out why he did it, won't that turn them into him? Won't they do it themselves? What about little Mishka? She's too young to understand. What about Saul? What if he turns really nasty the way Chase was? What about Valerie, what if she takes that hate he had?

Morgan was coughing deep coughs that forced their way up from the bottom of his lungs. He was holding his stomach with his hand-cuffed hands, curling up.

After what seemed like a long time, when he was actually coughing up blood, he stopped, and slumped, exhausted, on the back seat.

"Now," he said in a hoarse whisper. "Now we're going to close the door, okay? Close the door."

"Buddy?" Harley said, stooping to stare at him.

Morgan looked at him with bloodshot eyes, wiping his mouth on his pirate sleeve.

"You need a hospital or something?"

Morgan swallowed. "Glass of water?" he managed.

Harley ran inside and came out with a big paper cup of water. He climbed in the back seat with Morgan, pushed him upright, and held the cup to his lips. D.J. hugged herself, wondering if Chase would make a move: strangle Harley with the handcuffs, push the water in his face, and make a break. But Morgan sipped, coughed, sipped, sagged against the seat.

"Did you do it?" Harley asked.

"Yeah," said someone. It was hard to tell who, Morgan's voice was so strained. It sounded like it might be Gary. "You were right, Doro; couldn't take him in a fight, but when we went to—pull him inside us, the way Morgan does with ghosts, he came apart."

"Does this mean you're all—polluted by him?" she asked in a small voice.

211

"Ah, sugar," said Valerie, and took another sip of water. "Not like we didn't have our dark sides before."

"Are you going to kill people?" D.J. asked, her voice still high and tiny. She put her feet up on the seat and hugged her knees to her chest, her back against the passenger door.

"As the oldest, I took that part," Afra said, her voice clear. "I can own it without acting on it. Just as you could know about horrors and not become them. We have the power to say no."

"No more ghosts," Clift said.

"No more ghosts," agreed Elaine.

"You don't mind if I leave these cuffs on you for now, though, do you?" Harley asked.

"Cuffed me wrong," said Gary. "Should have done it behind my back, Buford."

"I know," said Harley.

"I don't mind," said Morgan. "Except I'd like breakfast."

"So would I," Harley said. "We've got to hang around here until the crime lab finishes, got to have our hands and guns tested—you know the routine, Gary—but I bet we could order something in." He went into the hotel office.

Morgan leaned forward, looking through the divider into D.J.'s eyes. She stared back, saw his eyes darken into Gary's. "Doro," he whispered. "I took the love."

"What?"

"They let me take what I could stand of him, and I took the love he had for you."

She closed her eyes. "I don't want that back."

"It's the cleanest thing he owned."

"Put it away, Gary." She stared into his eyes. "Whatever happens now, let that be just between us. All eleven of us, but—"

He took a deep breath, let it out. "All right," he said. "All right." He leaned back and relaxed against the seat. "As long as there's a future at all."

Was that possible? All the parts of Morgan she had begun to fall in love with, infected with pieces of what she most wanted to escape?

She looked at him. His eyes were closed and his breathing had slowed into sleep. She was tired of running away. She couldn't abandon him because he had followed her advice.

By the time Harley was back with food, she was thinking of ways to cover up spray-painted graffiti on apartment walls.

Egg Shells

Fern smoothed out her old shell, laid it on the bed, and patted it flat. Almost transparent, it looked faintly grayish pink, and it was as soft to the touch as camellia petals, faintly soapy.

She opened the room's in-chute and picked up the next shell. It glowed pale caramel and tingled with life.

For a moment she stared at her unshelled self in the mirror: awkward in the elbows and knees, so thin her bones showed white through her pale skin, eyes a rain-washed gray, buzz-cut hair a tarnished metal brown.

Fern had lived looking like that from the time she was born until she turned ten and started shelling three years earlier. She hated her base look.

Old holos of her mother looked like that: pale, thin, and bony. Her mother had been born too long ago to test-shell the way Fern and everyone she knew in school did. But Mom had picked a shell and changed after Fern was born. Mom had brown skin, white-blonde hair, and jewel green eyes now.

Fern opened the slit down the new shell's back and slid inside it. She stroked its surface until it attached to her own skin, then stood with her eyes closed while this shell changed her into someone else.

Oh yes. Much better. Her body filled out and grew muscular. She checked the mirror again. She looked strong. She lifted her chin and smiled at herself. Her skin had darkened to a coffee-with-cream shade, and her eyes had turned gold. Short fuzzy black hair capped her head. She touched it with newly dark fingers, liking the feel of its tight curls. The sensitivity in these fingers pleased her too.

She took a shower to get the new shell firmly settled. Water pounded it onto her, stapling it down.

While she showered, she got to know herself. Smooth dark skin with muscles just under the surface, a little boyish, pale palms and soles of the feet. Strange but good.

By the time she dried off, the old shell had dissolved into powder on the bed. She wished they wouldn't do that. She always forgot it was going to happen, and it made a mess. She stripped the bed and threw the pink-powdered sheets into the laundry chute.

"Fern?" Mother called from outside her door.

"Just a minute." Her new voice sounded warm and rich. She went to the in-chute and found a yellow dress, tossed it on over her head. It slid down and fitted perfectly. The clothes that showed up with new shells usually did. A small yellow pouch lay in the in-chute. Fern picked it up.

She put on underwear, but decided to skip socks.

"Fern? You're going to be late for the bus."

Fern slipped flat black shoes on, grabbed her carrypouch, dropped the yellow case into it, and dashed to the door.

"Oh!" said Mother.

Fern ran her hand over her short hair, ventured a smile.

Mother touched her cheek. "Lovely," she said in a faint voice.

Fern picked up her datacase by the front door. Its cover had shifted to yellow to match her dress. She slipped it into her carrypouch too.

The hoverbus was a little late. Just as well.

Sarah had saved her the same seat as always. Fern sat down, smoothing her skirt beneath her.

Sarah's new shell had big breasts and a perpetually

half-open mouth, with vivid red lips and small even teeth. Her new hair was long, curly, and blonde, and her new eyes were toffee-brown. She looked surprised.

Fern had worn a shell sort of like that a few shifts ago, and she had hated it.

Flipping her eyelashes, Sarah smiled. "Three boys tried to sit by me." She shrugged. "First time that's happened."

"What would happen if we didn't sit in the same place all the time?"

"Eww," said Sarah. "Don't. I wouldn't know you."

Fern peered into her carrypouch. She took out the yellow accessories pouch and tapped it open. A golden charm bracelet and small gold star earrings dropped out. "That would be weird," Fern said, fastening the bracelet around her left wrist, "but it might be interesting." She slipped the stars into holes in her ears.

Would they really not know each other? They had been best friends since kindergarten. No matter what shell Sarah wore, she always twisted her hair when she was puzzled or frustrated, and she sucked her bottom lip into her mouth when she was thinking hard. Sarah might be able to hide for a little while, but Fern was sure she'd figure out who Sarah was, given time.

She wasn't sure Sarah would know her back, though. Did Fern have habits that Sarah knew? Things she didn't even know she did?

"Puh-leeeeeze," Sarah said. "Don't go there. How would we get through the day?"

Fern looked at all the strangers on the bus. People she'd been going to school with for ages, but she didn't know who they were just yet, except for the ones who sat in the same seats all the time. Some people switched around a lot, especially the ones who didn't have friends. With new shells, they might be able to pretend to be interesting. Maybe they could fool somebody . . . until roll call in first class, anyway.

When she had started shelling three years ago, Fern had been totally confused every time everyone got new shells. She could memorize names and faces much faster now.

Sometimes people wore the same shells as long as a month. Sometimes they changed after two days. Most of the time, they spent a couple weeks in each shell. Fern didn't know she was going to change until she checked the alert light on the in-chute when she woke up each morning. If it was lit, there was a new shell to test.

Usually everybody changed shells on the same day. Once, about five of the boys had stayed in the same shells for another couple weeks, and Fern had felt strange and confused. She couldn't get herself to talk to them.

Fern took out her datacase and opened her shell journal. She made a few notes about what this shell looked like and how it felt. Then she jumped to the top of the file and peeked at her description of her first shell. Whoa. It seemed like ages ago. But it was only three years. How many shells had she had? She jumped down through the file. Some of them she couldn't even remember.

A boy two seats ahead of her turned and held up a small card with the name "Mica" on it. If he actually was Mica, he was shorter than he had been yesterday, and much thinner. He had long red hair and pale gray eyes.

Maybe it was someone else holding up a card with Mica's name on it. Fern frowned. The boy was sitting in Mica's seat. She might as well act as if he were Mica. She flickered two fingers at him, and he smiled.

Sarah nudged her. "Did you do the homework?"

Fern switched programs in her datacase. She couldn't remember doing her homework, but she always felt confused after changing shells. She tapped subject folders. Answer sheets scrolled down the screen, most of them filled out. Look at all the history, math, and science she had known yesterday. Or maybe she had just had a smart shell.

She slowed the scroll and stared at an equation for a little while, until her mind clicked and it made sense again. Some things left with the shells, and some things stayed with her.

"Let me see," Sarah said, reaching for the datacase.

Fern yawned and handed Sarah her answers. She flexed her arms, made muscles. They felt wonderful, sleek and powerful. Gym class would be so easy in this shell. Maybe Ms. Bark would say something nice.

Ms. Bark never seemed to follow anybody's transition from one shell to another. She was continually confused about who was who. She said, "You there—you're it. Dodge ball, everybody!" And, "Count off. Okay! Number one, you're the pitcher. Number three, you're the catcher . . ." Nobody got good grades in her class.

Sarah said Ms. Bark was one of those people who believed shelling was evil and refused to cooperate with it. Fern thought maybe Ms. Bark was too lazy to figure out who people were.

But every once in a while, she said something nice to an athletic shell. Finally Fern had one.

"Are you sure about this answer?" Sarah asked, pointing to an essay answer to a history question.

"Don't copy that," Fern said. "You can't have exactly the same answer as I do to an essay question, stupid. They'll know one of us is copying."

"I was going to put it in my own words, but it sounds wrong."

Fern glanced at the original question. *Why was the practice of shelling instituted?*

What a dumb question.

"When student uniformity could not be enforced through dress codes, and when shelling technology became available, it was thought . . ." Fern frowned at her own answer. Dumb question, dumber answer.

For a second she imagined an unshelled life. Stuck forever with that ugly wraith of a body.

At sixteen they would choose permanent shells. But they didn't have to choose the shells they were born with.

And if you paid a lot of money, you could switch again later on.

"This doesn't make sense," Sarah said. "If they want us to all be the same, how come we're all different all the time?"

"I think it was, like, they thought if we knew what it felt like to be a bunch of different people, we'd understand that we're all the same inside," Fern said, tensing and untensing her legs just because it felt so good and she liked watching the muscles ripple and release beneath the smooth dark skin. "I don't get it. It didn't make sense in the textfile, either."

"So you're just saying back?"

"Uh huh."

Their teachers didn't like them to parrot textfiles. But it was good enough for a C, and sometimes Fern just didn't care about the material.

"I'll make something up," Sarah said. She tapped her keyboard.

One of the boys behind them leaned forward and stared at Sarah's new breasts. He licked his lips.

"Eww," cried Sarah, shrinking away from him.

"Yum," he said. He widened his eyes.

"Cut it out, Cody," Fern said, shoving the boy's head back.

"I'm not Cody," he said. He was dark-haired and freckle-splattered, with narrow blue eyes and lots of large teeth.

"Sure you are. This wasn't funny last time, either."

"I'm not Cody," he repeated.

Fern stared at him, trying to figure out if he was kidding. She glanced at everybody in the bus, and for a dizzying moment, all their faces meshed and melted and swam and reformed, until she thought she didn't know anyone. What if she got on the wrong bus one day and couldn't even tell?

What if Sarah wasn't Sarah?

Fern sat and let possibilities shudder through her. It was scary. Was everybody actually the same inside? Didn't your shell shape you? Sometimes she knew things in one shell she forgot in another. And for sure the boys had been a lot different to her when she had had big breasts. Once she had had a fat shell, and that had been different too. People looked away from her. Some teachers ignored her, even when her desk answer light was lit.

Today she felt strong and beautiful. Yesterday she had been in a really normal shell, and everything had been ordinary.

Lots of people chose ordinary shells for their ultimate shells. Why?

"Hey, lady," said the not-Cody boy, still staring at Sarah's chest, "I want some of that."

Maybe he really wasn't Cody. Cody had never said anything so gross.

Or maybe his shell was making him act different?

Maybe boy shells did that. Boys always got boy shells, and girls always got girl shells. Somebody said they were working on cross-gender shells, but it was a much more complicated technology and would take a while to develop. Fern imagined her own children switching sexes and looks every couple of weeks.

How would you know to love them? What if the children came home to the wrong house one day? What if no one could tell?

Fern glared at the freckle-faced boy. "It doesn't matter who you are," she said. "Just quit it!" She pushed him again. His eyes got slittier, but he sat back.

Fern glanced at Sarah, who sniffled a little bit. So she didn't like that kind of attention either. Another shock of dislocation shuddered through Fern as she wondered whether this actually *was* Sarah.

Whoever she is, she thinks she's my best friend, Fern thought. She smelled the back of her own hand. It smelled alien, cinnamon and strange.

She hesitated, then set her hand on the seat cushion between her and Sarah.

Sarah's surprised blue eyes looked at Fern's face, then down at her hand. Sarah sucked her bottom lip into her mouth for ten seconds, then put her hand down next to Fern's.

They meshed fingers and pressed palm to palm.

Whoever you are, your hand is warm, Fern thought, *and thank you.*

About the Author

Nina Kiriki Hoffman has sold more than 200 stories, five adult novels, and a number of juvenile and media tie-in works. Her short stories and novels have been finalists for the Science Fiction Writers of America Nebula award, the World Fantasy Award, and the Endeavor Award. Her novel *The Thread That Binds The Bones* won a Horror Writers Association Bram Stoker Award for first novel, and her short story "A Step into Darkness" won a Writers of the Future Award. Her available books include *The Silent Strength of Stones* from Avon and *A Red Heart of Memories*, *Past the Size of Dreaming*, and *A Fistful of Sky from Ace*. A young adult novel (title currently undergoing revision) will come out in hardcover from Viking in 2003.

In addition to writing, Nina works at B. Dalton Bookstore one afternoon a week, does production work for *The Magazine of Fantasy & Science Fiction*, copyedits novels for the Gale Group, and teaches short story writing through Lane Community College's continuing education program.

Nina lives in Eugene with cats and a mannequin. Her anime collection keeps growing.